A hOuSe DiViDeD

the misadventures of Willie Plummet

PAUL BUCHANAN & ROD RANDALL

CPH
SAINT LOUIS

The Misadventures of Willie Plummet

Invasion from Planet X
Submarine Sandwiched
Anything You Can Do I Can Do Better
Ballistic Bugs
Battle of the Bands
Gold Flakes for Breakfast
Tidal Wave
Shooting Stars
Hail to the Chump
The Monopoly
Heads I Win, Tails You Lose
Ask Willie
Stuck on You
Dog Days
Brain Freeze
Friend or Foe
Don't Rock the Float
Face the Music
Lock-In
A House Divided

Cover illustration by John Ward.
Back cover photo by Ira Lippke.
Cover and interior design by Karol Bergdolt.

Scripture quotations are taken from the HOLY BIBLE, NEW INTERNATIONAL VERSION®. NIV®. Copyright ©1973, 1978, 1984 by International Bible Society. Used by permission of Zondervan Publishing House. All rights reserved.

Copyright © 2001 Paul Buchanan
Published by Concordia Publishing House
3558 S. Jefferson Avenue, St. Louis, MO 63118-3968

Manufactured in the United States of America

Library of Congress Cataloging-in-Publication Data

Buchanan, Paul.
    A house divided / Paul Buchanan, Rod Randall.
       p. cm. — (The misadventures of Willie Plummet)
      Summary: When Willie's family acquires a second hobby store in Cedarville, he needs God's help making a difficult decision that he knows will be best for everyone.
    ISBN 0-570-07131-3
      [1. Stores, Retail—Fiction. 2. Family life—Fiction. 3. Friendship—Fiction.
4. Christian life—Fiction.] I. Randall, Rod, 1962- II. Title.
II. Title.
    PZ7.B87717 Ho 2001
    [Fic]—dc21

1 2 3 4 5 6 7 8 9 10   10 09 08 07 06 05 04 03 02 01

For Phil Behm,
Sean Wallace,
and Mike Harvey,
all great dinner companions.

Contents

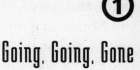

When Dad and Mr. Paulson went out the front door for a stroll after dinner, it didn't strike me as odd. I helped Mom carry the dishes in from the dinner table, and as I piled them in the sink, I saw the two men walking down the driveway away from me. Mr. Paulson gestured with his hands as he spoke. Dad walked beside him, his hands linked behind his back, his head low, listening intently.

But it didn't seem odd to me, and when I was done helping Mom, I just went in the living room and switched on the television.

We'd had Mr. Paulson over for dinner before. He was a big, jovial man who had a habit of laughing himself red-faced and then dabbing his forehead with his handkerchief while he caught his breath. If I'd been more observant that night, I might have noticed that he laughed very little over dinner and that Dad had fallen silent a few times, staring into the middle distance and losing track of the conversation.

Something big was happening in the adult world, and I—as usual—was clueless.

I'm 13 years old, and the world of adults doesn't often make sense to me. Why do grown-ups spend hours driving to the beach only to sit under an umbrella and look at the waves? Why do they watch the news every night on TV, when they could watch the Animaniacs? Why do they worry so much about things they have no control over?

When the show I was watching was over, Dad and Mr. Paulson still hadn't come back from their walk. I switched off the television and went back in the kitchen to make a phone call.

Mom was done cleaning up, but my big sister, Amanda, sat at the kitchen table filling out yet another application for yet another college. She'd be graduating from high school in May, and she dreamed of going off to college and leaving us all behind— although Dad kept warning her not to get her hopes too high. With family finances the way they were, she might have to spend a couple of years at Glenfield Community College.

My family runs Plummet Hobbies, a shop down on Main Street. We do a pretty good business. It's paid the bills over the years, but we're nowhere close to being rich—and college tuition isn't cheap.

When I picked up the phone, Amanda began frantically erasing something she'd written on one of the applications—and then she glared at me, as if it was somehow my fault.

"Do you have to do that in here?" she said. "This is very important. I really want to go to college."

Believe me, I really wanted her to go to college too—preferably a distant one. The University of Northern Siberia sounded good to me. "I'm just making a phone call," I told her. "I don't think that's going to keep you out of Yale."

"Look, I'm trying to concentrate," she said. "Can't you take the phone somewhere else?"

I had been trying to call Felix, one of my two best friends, since school had let out that day, but his line was always busy. He must be on the Internet, I thought. That was Felix's latest obsession—the latest in a string of many. Every few weeks, Felix discovered something that fascinated him so much he was practically taken hostage by it. He went through astronomy, stamp collecting, and chess—which were at least normal pastimes. It was much harder to explain his obsessions with soap making, handwriting analysis, and worm farming.

Now Felix was on an Internet kick, and he was always telling us about places he'd found on the world wide web where you could get instructions on how to make your own ketchup or a complete list of the places where Alfred Hitchcock appeared in his own movies.

"All this stuff is totally useless," I'd tell him. "Why would I want to make my own ketchup?"

He'd just shake his head, like I was impossibly naive. "Once you've tasted homemade, you can never go back," he'd assure me.

I took the cordless phone from the kitchen to the computer room that Dad used as an office and dialed Felix's number again. This time he answered the phone on the third ring.

"I've only got a few minutes," he said as soon as he realized it was me. "I've got to get back on line."

"Felix, can't you just give it a rest?" I said. "We hardly ever see you anymore. What could be so important that you have to get right back on line?"

"I'm in a fierce bidding war on eBay with some guy in British Columbia," he told me. "The auction is over in half an hour, and I want to make sure he doesn't outbid me in the closing minutes."

"Really?" I said. It actually sounded pretty exciting. "What are you bidding for?"

There was a pause on the other end of the line. "We're bidding on a kilt," Felix said.

"Come again?"

"A kilt," he said. "You know, like in Scotland."

"You're trying to buy a kilt?" I said. "What do you want with a kilt?"

"It's my size," he told me, as if that was some kind of explanation. "And it's a real bargain."

I stood there in the computer room, holding the phone to my ear, blinking. "But it's a *kilt*."

"It's real Scottish wool," he assured me. "And it comes with its own sporran. Do you have any idea how expensive it would be if I bought it new?"

I didn't even bother to ask what a sporran was; it was knowledge I could probably do without. "So how much are you paying for this piece of cutting-edge fashion?" I asked him.

"Six dollars and thirty-five cents, plus shipping and handling," Felix told me proudly. "Can you believe it?" His voice dropped to a whisper. "Unless that MacTavish guy in Canada outbids me."

I sighed and shook my head. "Well, I hope you win," I told Felix. "No one named MacTavish has any right to buy your kilt."

"Thanks, Dude," Felix told me, oblivious to my sarcasm. "I'll let you know tomorrow how it pans out."

"It's going to be hard getting to sleep tonight," I told him.

"I know it," he said breathlessly. "Gotta go." He hung up.

I pushed the button on my phone that hung it up and stood there a moment trying to picture Felix in a kilt. The weird thing was, it actually looked pretty good on him.

I took the phone back in the kitchen and set it in its cradle—quietly, so I wouldn't keep Amanda out of college.

When Dad came back from his walk, he and Mr. Paulson stood out on the front porch talking a while longer. I could see their shadows from where I sat watching television, and I could hear their voices, though I couldn't make out what they were saying. Eventually they shook hands, and Dad stood on the porch alone while Mr. Paulson backed his car out of the drive and drove out of sight. Dad stood there on the porch a few more minutes, but still it didn't occur to me to wonder what was going on. I was too immersed in what I was watching. I was just a kid.

Dad finally came inside and Mom followed him back to his office. They closed the door, but I could hear them in there talking. I was too busy watching TV to wonder what they were talking about.

At lunch the next day, I got my tray of food and stood looking around the Glenfield Middle School cafeteria for Sam and Felix. We always ate lunch together.

I saw Sam sitting at an empty table in the back. Her full name is Samantha, but we all call her Sam.

She's my other best friend. When she noticed me coming toward her, she smiled and waved. I went over and put my tray down across from hers. She was holding a little blue automatic camera, and by the whirring sound, I could tell that the film was finished and was winding back into its canister.

I bowed my head and said grace, and when I opened my eyes again, Felix was there. He slid his tray next to Sam's and sat down.

"What's the camera for?" Felix asked.

"It's for the yearbook," Sam told us. "Not enough people turned in those candid shots that get put in all over the place—and we've got to send the yearbook out in a couple of weeks or we'll never get it back in time for the end of school."

"Well, why don't you take some shots of me?" Felix said, suddenly full of energy. "It'll make me look like one of the popular kids."

Sam replaced the roll of film and closed the back of the camera. "I'm afraid that would take more than a photo," she told him. She bent and slipped her camera into her backpack.

"I think Felix is well on the way to becoming one of the popular kids," I told her straight-faced. "Just wait till he comes to school wearing his sleek new kilt. That's going to turn some heads."

"Kilt?" Sam said.

Felix sat up straight, suddenly energized again. "Dude," he said. "That MacTavish guy stole it out from under me in the closing seconds of the auction."

"Kilt?" Sam said again.

"Felix tried to buy a kilt on eBay last night," I told her, grinning. "Real Scottish wool. It came with its own sporran."

"Sporran?" Sam said.

I shrugged. I still had no idea what one was.

Felix stared over my head, like an old man about to tell a war story. "It was so close I could taste it," he said dramatically. "I could practically smell all the Scottish sheep that gave their wool to make it."

I winced. It wasn't a particularly appealing expression, especially at lunch.

He held one fist in the air in front of his face. "And then MacTavish in Canada upped it another 75 cents in the final seconds, and by the time I—"

"Wait," Sam interrupted. "What could you possibly want with a kilt?"

"It was my size," he told her. He obviously hadn't come up with a better explanation since I talked to him last night.

Sam laughed. "So if there was a straightjacket your size, you'd bid on it?"

Felix sighed wearily. "Very funny," he said. "I don't *need* a straightjacket."

"Believe me," Sam said. "You need one more than a kilt."

When school let out, Felix, Sam, and I walked over to my house. Sam had just got out of her sixth period yearbook elective class.

"Do you have any idea how far behind we are?" she asked as we passed by Lawton Park. "We've only got a few weeks to get it to the printer and all we've got done is the eighth grade section. I don't know what we're going to do."

At the beginning of the school year, Sam had signed on to be the assistant editor of the yearbook. But the editor-in-chief moved away to California, so Sam had to take over. Then, not long after Christmas, two of her photographers joined a softball team and quit. It seemed like the whole yearbook had fallen on Sam's shoulders—and with the end of the school year quickly approaching, she was getting pretty anxious about it.

"Chill out," Felix told her. "It's just a stupid year book. You pass them out, we write all over them, we put them on a shelf, and they collect dust. It's no big deal."

Sam stopped walking and put her hands on her hips. She looked offended. "It *is* a big deal," Sam told Felix. "You may not care right now, but someday you'll appreciate this yearbook. Someday you'll want to remember all this." Sam made a sweeping gesture with her arm that seemed to take in the whole town of Glenfield.

"Trust me," Felix said. "There's nothing about this stupid place I'll want to remember. A case of complete amnesia would suit me fine." He'd been in a bad mood all day—probably because of the kilt.

Sam just shook her head and started walking again. She knew it was no use arguing with him. Felix and I fell into step beside her.

While we walked, I looked around at the houses we passed and the big trees that touched branches over the middle of the street. Glenfield wasn't much of a town, I had to admit. But I knew I'd miss it if I ever had to leave. And I was pretty sure Felix would too.

When the three of us got to my house, Mom's car wasn't in the driveway and the front door was locked. That was unusual. Mom was almost always there when I got home.

I got out my key and opened the door. The three of us went inside. While I stooped to pick up the mail on the entry floor, Felix made a beeline to the kitchen. "Food," he chanted. "I need food." I set the mail on the hallway table, and Sam and I followed Felix into the kitchen.

I got a loaf of bread and was setting it on the kitchen table when I noticed Mom's note attached to the freezer with a magnet. I pulled it off.

> Willie,
> Your dad and I went into cedarville on business. We'll be back before dinner.
> Love, Mom
>
> P.S. Don't let Felix eat all the sliced turkey. It's for your dad's lunches.

I slipped the note in the back pocket of my jeans and looked at Felix. His head was buried in the refrigerator up to the shoulders. He dug around on the bottom shelf humming a tune. He finally stopped humming and straightened up to look at me. "Got any more of those turkey slices?" he wanted to know.

I was halfway through my peanut butter sandwich when the doorbell rang. I went to the front door and looked through the peephole. It was Phoebe, my next door neighbor. She's about 10-years-old, and she goes to Grove Street Elementary School—the same school I used to go to. She held some kind of envelope in her hand.

Phoebe was a sweet girl, but she was a total pest. She was always coming over and trying to hang out with us, and—to make it worse—she'd had a crush on me for as long as I could remember. I pulled the door halfway open and stood in the doorway, so it wouldn't look like I was inviting her in.

"Hey, Pheeb," I said. "What's up?"

"Not much," she said. She tried to see around me to find out whether Sam and Felix were there, but I just stood in her way. She looked up at me. "I saw your mom and dad leaving when I came home for lunch. I just wanted to make sure everything was okay."

"Everything's fine," I told her. "They just went into Cedarville for something."

"You mean they closed up the store during business hours?"

I shrugged. "I guess," I said. "Is there anything I can do for you?"

"I was just wondering—"

"*Dude*," Felix said. I jumped. I hadn't heard him come up behind me. He put his hand on my shoulder and pulled me away from the door. He waved something in my face. "I thought you said there was no turkey. I found a whole package under the broccoli in the vegetable drawer. Hey, Phoebe."

It was too late. Phoebe had slipped through the door and was following Felix back to the kitchen—

where he would no doubt offer to make her a turkey sandwich.

About an hour later, through the kitchen window, we heard Phoebe's mom finally calling her. We all looked at Phoebe. She sighed. Mean as it sounds, I was relieved that she'd be going.

"That's a shame," I said. "Do you have to leave so soon?"

Phoebe said her reluctant good-byes to each of us and trudged out through the swinging kitchen door. A few seconds later, from the kitchen window, I saw her cross the lawn between our houses and disappear.

"Hey, what's this?" Felix said. He'd just sat down at the table across from me with his third turkey sandwich. He was reading a sheet of paper that he'd found lying next to an open manila envelope. "Phoebe must have left this," he said. "It's the results of her end-of-the-year testing." His eyes darted across the page. "Man," he said. "That girl's *smart*." He picked the page up so he could read it better.

"I don't think Phoebe wanted you to see that," Sam told Felix.

"But she just left it lying here," Felix said defensively. He was tilting his head now and squinting at the fine print.

"Yeah," I said. "But it's private. We're not supposed to be looking at it."

Sam snatched the paper from Felix's hands. "As I was saying," she went on. "I don't think she wanted you to see it." She turned and held it in front of my face. "She obviously wanted *Willie* to see it."

"What?" I said, beginning to blush. "Why would she want *me* to see it?" The bar graphs on the sheet of paper looked like the Manhattan skyline. All Phoebe's scores were nearly perfect.

"Oh, come on, Willie," Sam said. "That poor girl's been trying to impress you for years."

I blushed deeper. "She has *not*," I said. "She just left it behind on accident." I pushed Sam's arm out of the way, got up, and took my plate to the kitchen sink.

When I turned back around, Sam was smiling at me. "I think it's cute how she adores you," Sam said. "You should take it as a compliment."

"It's no compliment," I said. "I never asked for her to have a crush on me. It's totally embarrassing." I brushed past Sam and took my seat at the table again.

"Willie has a girlfriend. Willie has a girlfriend," Felix chanted like a kindergartner. "Willie has a girlfriend."

I leaned forward and looked him in the eye. "Can you buy crutches on eBay?" I asked him.

After Sam and Felix left, I went upstairs and started my homework. Around dinnertime, I heard the front door open and shut. I assumed it was Mom and Dad—but a few seconds later I heard a scream.

I jumped up from my desk, toppling my chair backward, and sprinted down the stairs, flushed with adrenaline. When I got to the front hallway, I saw Amanda there, hopping around and squealing as if she were on fire.

"What's wrong?" I sputtered. "What happened?"

Amanda looked at me and screamed again. She lunged at me and got me in a bear hug before I could stop her, and then she began jumping up and down again, still squeezing me tight.

"Are you nuts?" I said, trying to push her away from me. "What's the matter with you? Let go of me."

Amanda took a step back, looked at me, and squealed again. She reached out at me and I ducked—but she was only trying to show me what had come in the mail for her. It was a letter on one sheet of white stationery, and she frantically waved it in the air between us.

"They *took* me," she squealed. "Midland University accepted me! They were my first choice."

She tried to hug me again, but I was too fast for her this time. I backed up a few steps. So instead of hugging me, she just did a little dance on the hallway floor.

I laughed and shook my head. "I thought you were on fire," I told her from a safe distance. "Imagine my disappointment."

She just laughed and hugged the letter to her chest. "I'm going to college, little brother," she said, once she'd caught her breath. "I'm actually going to college."

I laughed again. "That's great," I told her. "That's really great."

Amanda looked down at the letter again. I watched her bright eyes move back and forth over the page. Her face beamed with happiness. "Don't you *dare* breathe a word of this to Mom and Dad," she warned me. "I want to tell them."

Back in my room, sitting at my desk, I tried to do my homework, but it was hard to concentrate. I wasn't sure how to feel for Amanda. It was good to see her so happy, but in a way I felt sorry for her. It looked like she was headed for a fall. She'd been accepted at her top pick college, but I was pretty sure my parents couldn't afford to send her.

I cradled my face in my hands and stared down at my open math book. Amanda was in love with the idea of going off to college—and if she went, she'd be the first Plummet to do it. For months now, she'd sat at the dinner table, talking about nothing but SAT scores, admission essays, and entrance requirements. State College had a very good nursing program, she'd tell us—as if this were fascinating mealtime conversation—but Midland University had the best overall reputation.

As she spoke, Dad would just look down at his plate and poke at his food with his fork. I knew he was worried about the money, but he hated to dampen Amanda's enthusiasm. Sometimes Mom would say good things about Glenfield Community College—about how it was a good place to get the fundamentals before you transferred to a big university—but Amanda never seemed to get the hint.

When I heard the car pull into the driveway, I got up from the desk and looked out my bedroom window. I watched Dad and Mom get out of the car and walk up to the house. Dad already looked anxious and worried. I hated to think how he'd look once he heard Amanda's news.

Dinner was about an hour and a half later than usual that night. The smell of cooking beef rose through the house while I sat at my desk and tried to finish my homework. I was really hungry.

When Mom finally called us all downstairs, I paused outside Amanda's room and knocked on her door. She opened it a crack and looked out at me. Her face was still radiant with happiness.

"Have you told them yet?" I asked her, hoping she had.

She grinned and shook her head. "I thought I'd tell them all at dinner," she said. "I want it to be a surprise."

I kept the smile on my face, but I felt my stomach twist into a knot—the last thing I wanted was to be sitting in the audience when Amanda's dreams were crushed. "See you downstairs," I told her and pulled her bedroom door shut.

When I got down to the dining room, I was surprised to find a platter of steaks on the table instead of meatloaf. Steak was only for important occasions—had Mom figured out Amanda's news? Was this some kind of consolation meal to make Amanda feel less bad?

I sat down at my place at the table and waited for the others.

While Dad said grace—and it was unusually long tonight—I could hear Amanda across from me, squirming in her seat. As soon as I raised my head and opened my eyes, I looked over at Dad. He seemed tired. He took a deep breath and gathered himself up. He looked like he was about to make an announcement, but Amanda beat him to it.

"They *took* me!" she squealed, unable to hold in her excitement a second longer. "Midland University accepted me! I'm a college girl."

I saw Mom dart a look at Dad. He looked down at his plate a long time, as if contemplating where to make the first cut in his steak. He finally raised his head, nodded silently and then looked around at each of us.

"I have some news too," he said, softly and deliberately. "Something important has happened."

He looked so grave and serious, even Amanda fell suddenly silent. I glanced at Mom. She nodded, and I put down my knife and fork to listen.

"We all need to talk about something very serious," he said. "The five of us have to make a big decision."

I leaned forward. I could suddenly feel my heart beating.

"Mr. Paulson has decided to retire from the hobby business," Dad went on. "He's got a thriving shop over in Cedarville, and he hates to do it, but he says it's time to retire."

"Wow," Orville said. "That's got to be good for our shop. He's our closest competitor. If he closes up, we'll be the only hobby shop in the whole tri-county area."

Dad nodded. "Well, closing up his shop is one possibility," he said. "Mr. Paulson is actually hoping that we'll buy his business. He wants us to take over his shop as well as ours."

I let out the breath I'd been holding. The way Dad had been acting, I'd been expecting bad news, but this was great news—wasn't it?

"Mr. Paulson made me an offer when he was over here for dinner," Dad continued. "He's willing to sell Hobby City to us for practically nothing because he likes the way we do business."

That's why the two of them took that walk, I thought. *That's* why Dad's been so serious the last few days.

"I've been looking at the books," Dad went on. "And his store makes a lot more money than ours at this point. It's in a bigger town, and it has a lot more space. If we take it over, we might have enough money to send the three of you off to college." He looked across the table at Mom. "And your mom and I can finally put some money away for retirement."

"Midland University, here I come!" Amanda squealed.

Dad smiled wearily. "Yes," he said. "But we all have to agree that we should take on the new store. It'll be a lot of hard work, and all of us will have to chip in. God made us a family, and this is a family decision. The whole family has to agree on it."

I looked at Orville and Amanda. They were both grinning.

"How can we help?" I asked Dad.

"Well, your mother and I have been talking about it," Dad said. "At first I'll probably have to spend most of my time at the new store. I'll have to learn the business, and then—if we make enough money—maybe I can hire a store manager to keep it going."

"So who's going to run *our* store?" Orville asked. It was a good question.

"Well, we were thinking your mother could spend more time there—while you three are at school," Dad said. "Willie, you can help her after school and Orville can come over right after baseball practice."

"What about me?" Amanda wanted to know. "What can I do?"

"Well, it looks like you'll be heading off to Midland University in a few months," Dad said. "But until then, you'll have to pull your weight too. We were thinking you could sort of cover for your mother at home till we get things all worked out."

"Anything," Amanda said, fidgeting with excitement. "I'll do anything."

Dad smiled. He still looked a little worried, but he was obviously proud of Amanda. He looked around the table. "All in favor?" he asked.

All five of us immediately raised our hands.

Early Saturday morning, Dad pulled the car into the Hobby City parking lot in Cedarville. He shut off the engine, and we all just sat there silently in the car, our seat belts still buckled, looking up at the building.

I'd been to Hobby City a few times before. Dad liked to stop in there to see Mr. Paulson anytime we were in Cedarville, and the visits were usually pretty dull. I'd roam around the store a bit, while Dad and Mr. Paulson stood on either side of the glass counter talking shop. When it got too boring, I'd go out to look at the other stores in the same strip mall. But now that we were looking up at the building—a building we actually now owned—I realized how little I remembered it.

Dad finally opened his car door and stepped outside, and the rest of us followed. The building was all closed up. Dad pulled the key from his pocket, and we crowded around as he unlocked the door. I'd brought along my camera, and I had it slung around my neck.

"Wait," I said, before he could pull the door open. "Let me get a picture of this." I stepped out into the parking lot and backed up until I could get the whole front of the store in the picture. Mom and Dad and Amanda and Orville looked dwarfed by the huge storefront. "Smile," I told them—even though I was so far away, their smiles probably wouldn't show up in the picture.

"You should be in the picture too," Mom told me.

"Yeah," Dad said. "Let's get the whole family."

I walked back to the car and balanced the camera on the trunk. I bent over and squinted through the viewfinder and adjusted the camera until the picture looked right. Then I set the timer and ran over to join the others.

I stood there next to my dad, grinning like an idiot, until the shutter clicked.

The store was dark and cool inside, and none of us knew where the light switch was. For a while we shuffled around in the shadows until Mom found the switch and the fluorescent lights over head blinked on. In the sudden light, we all fell silent again.

I stood in the long central aisle, and I was struck for the first time by how large the store was. Steel shelving and tiled floors gleamed in the overhead light. Aisle after aisle branched off in both directions. A long glass case ran all the way along the side wall, turned the corner and ran along the back wall as well. A security camera was mounted high above the computerized cash register. By the door stood a rack of red plastic shopping baskets, each with the Hobby City logo. It seemed so big and modern and bright—nothing like our old plank-floored shop back home.

"I'd forgotten how big this place is," I said.

Dad laughed. "Me too," he admitted.

He went over to the gap in the glass case and slipped behind the counter to try out the view. He looked excited and happy back there. He smiled and patted the glass counter with his palms. I raised the camera to my eye and snapped a photo of him standing there.

We were about a half-hour from Glenfield, out on the highway, cruising past farms and fruit stands on our way home from Hobby City. Dad was excited and talkative, and the rest of us just sat smiling and listening to him. He was talking about train set displays when we came up on the billboard. I felt the car slow suddenly.

It was an advertisement for Hobby City—but the panels of paper were peeling off like old wallpaper. It showed a big, faded picture of the inside of the store and Mr. Paulson standing in the center aisle with his arms spread out. On the base of the billboard, it said Tri-County Advertising.

"Is that our billboard now?" Orville asked

Dad looked at Mom. "I guess so," he said. "I never thought to check."

"Well, if it's ours, we should get it fixed up," Orville said, as we passed the billboard. "That should be *you* up there trying to hug everyone."

Dad laughed. "It's not just my store," Dad said. "It belongs to the whole family. We're all going to be working hard."

I twisted and looked out the back window. It had the same advertisement on the other side as well—just as faded and peeling.

I turned back around and faced forward. I looked out at all the traffic on the highway—even on a weekend, thousands of cars must pass that billboard every day.

When we got back to our house, Felix, Sam, and Phoebe were all lined up sitting on the curb looking bored. They got up when we pulled into the driveway.

"We were in Cedarville to look at the new store," I told them when I got out of the car. "You should see the place; it's huge."

"Is that the camera Mrs. Lawson gave you?" Sam wanted to know.

I looked down at the camera that hung around my neck on its strap. "Yeah," I said. "I wanted to get some pictures of the new store."

"Cool," Sam said.

I looked down at the camera. The pointer said it was on shot 35. "Hey, there's one more shot on this roll of film," I said. "If you guys have nothing to do, why don't we finish up this roll and turn it in at the photo shop?"

I set the camera on the hood of the car, which was hot from our drive, and directed Sam and Felix and Phoebe to pose on the porch steps. When everything was ready, I set the timer and ran over to join them. We draped our arms over each other's shoulders and grinned at the camera until the shutter clicked.

Soup's On (Fire)

"How's the yearbook coming?" I asked Sam the next Monday after I sat down across from her in the cafeteria and said grace. She had been carrying her camera with her everywhere at school that day. She looked tired and anxious.

"It's driving me crazy," she admitted. She rested her forehead on one hand and used the other to poke at her macaroni with her fork. "But if we can just get it all done and off to the printer in a couple of weeks, we can have it in everybody's hands six weeks from now when school lets out."

"And seven weeks from now, it'll be on the shelf collecting dust," Felix said. "Nobody cares." He crammed a forkful of macaroni into his mouth and began to chew.

Sam glared at him. I knew she was frustrated. She was working hard to make the best yearbook she could. I wanted to stick up for her.

"Speaking of collecting dust," I said. "How is that pasta maker you bought on eBay?"

Felix swallowed. "Hey, lay off," he whined. "You've never even been on eBay. There's plenty of valuable stuff out there that's dirt cheap."

"Like that cookie jar you bought that's shaped like Elvis's head?" Sam chimed in. It was good to see her smiling again.

"Hey, that's a limited edition," Felix informed her. "It's sure to appreciate in value. And there's plenty more investments where that came from."

"Yeah, like what?" I began to open my little carton of milk.

Felix glanced around the cafeteria and then leaned in closer, like he was about to tell us a secret. "Well, I *do* have a bid in on the world's largest egg timer."

I set down my not-yet-open milk carton and looked at him. "The world's largest egg timer?" I said. This was bizarre even for Felix.

"I'm the only bidder so far. I could get it for $9 plus shipping and handling," he said. "If there are no other bidders between now and Thursday afternoon, that is."

"No sign of MacTavish on this one?" Sam asked. She winked at me.

"So far MacTavish is nowhere in sight," Felix said gravely.

"So what do you want with the world's largest egg timer?" I asked him.

"Dude, it's a world's record."

"So?" Sam said.

"I'll be the only person in town with a world's record," Felix said. "It's got to be worth more than $9. Do you have any idea what the world's largest diamond is worth?"

"That's not the best analogy you've ever made," Sam told him. "A diamond is a precious jewel. An egg timer—well, it's an *egg* timer."

I laughed.

Felix crammed another forkful of macaroni in his mouth and chewed smugly. He swallowed and took a sip of milk. "Just wait," Felix said. "We'll see who's laughing at who when I put Glenfield on the map with a world-record egg timer."

"I'd prefer to start laughing at you now, if it's all the same to you," Sam told him.

At five o'clock, Mom turned around the sign in the front window from OPEN to CLOSED and locked the door. Our first business day without Dad was complete, and we were both exhausted. I got the broom from the back room and swept the floor, while

Mom closed out the cash register, counted up the money, and put it in the safe. I was done in 15 minutes.

For a while Mom and I just sat on the stools behind the counter, tired and sore, waiting for Dad to show up. Mom seemed happy with herself. She'd done it. She'd run the whole business for a whole day, and judging by the cash register totals, we'd done pretty well.

"If your dad closed up the store in Cedarville at 5, and got on the highway at a quarter after, he should be here around 6:30," Mom said looking at her watch. "Why don't you go on home, and I'll wait for him? At least you can get started on your homework."

"Sure," I said. "You don't mind waiting on your own?"

"There's plenty I can do here until your father arrives," Mom said. "Go on home, and stay out of your sister's way. She said she'd have dinner ready around seven."

When I came up the drive, the front door was wide open. I went inside and pulled the door shut behind me. The house seemed to be filled with a light fog. The smoke alarm in the back hallway blared loudly. And then I smelled something like burned toast. I pushed the front door open again and went to the kitchen door. Curls of smoke leaked out through the crack beneath the door. I pushed the door open. Thicker smoke billowed out at me.

"I can explain," a shrill voice came out of the smoke—and then it erupted into a fit of coughing. A dim figure came toward me through the smoke. "Oh, it's just you," Amanda said. "Where's Mom?" She turned on her heels and disappeared into the smoke again.

"She's still at the store," I said. I propped the kitchen door open with a chair so the smoke could escape out the front door.

In a few seconds I could make Amanda out. She was standing at the sink, trying to fan the smoke out the kitchen window with a dishtowel. "What did you *do* in here?" I asked her.

"I have everything under control," she told me curtly. She stopped flapping the towel a moment to glare at me. "And I don't want to hear any of your stupid jokes."

I laughed. She'd read my mind. "Oh, come on," I said. "I've already thought of three good ones."

"No jokes," she said. "Just get out of the kitchen." She put the dishtowel down long enough to come over and push me out the kitchen door. "Go away, and don't you dare tell Mom about this." She pulled out the chair I'd placed in the doorway. The kitchen door swung shut, but wisps of smoke still curled out around the edges.

I went out to the garage and found the fans we'd be using when summer came. I dusted one off with a rag and took it into the kitchen.

"I told you not to come in here," Amanda whined, but then she saw the fan in my hands. "Good idea," she said.

I set it up on the kitchen counter, and aimed it out the open kitchen window. I turned it to high, and watched as the smoke got sucked outside.

"Okay," Amanda said. "That's much better. Now get out of the kitchen."

I went and sat on the front porch with my social studies book. Even with the kitchen door closed, I could see smoke seeping under the front door as I read. Eventually the smoke alarm turned itself off—or maybe the batteries just wore out.

"There's a bunch of smoke coming out of your house," a high voice said.

I looked up from my book to see Phoebe coming across the lawn toward me. I closed my book and set it on the porch beside me. "It's Amanda," I said. "She's cooking dinner. *Chicken a la Arson.*" It was one of the three jokes I'd thought of, but it didn't even get a snicker. Phoebe just stood on the lawn at the bottom of the porch steps looking down at her feet. She seemed a little distracted.

"Your sister's doing the cooking?" Phoebe asked, finally looking at me. "I thought she was a really bad cook."

"She is," I said. "But with Mom running the hobby shop, it's either Amanda's cooking or starvation. The vote was three to two."

Phoebe didn't even smile. She just nodded. It was clear she had something on her mind. She bit her lower lip and looked down at the lawn again. "Well," she said. "I bet you'll be really hungry for a good meal in a week or two."

"I'm hungry for a good meal now," I said. "But what are the chances?"

"I'll bet you'd love to go to some kind of big banquet a couple of weeks from now," Phoebe said. The topic of food seemed to have made her very nervous.

"What are you getting at, Pheeb?" I asked her. "You're acting even weirder than usual."

"Nothing," she said, flustered. "I'm not getting at anything. I'm just making conversation."

"You're up to something," I said. "Why not just get to the point?"

Phoebe sighed. She plucked up a blade of grass and nervously wound it around her finger like a ring. "Well there is something," she admitted. "Now that you mention it."

"Spit it out," I told her.

"Well, it's like this," she said. "I was named student of the year at Grove Street Elementary School."

I looked at her. Phoebe was always trying to impress me. Why had it been so hard for her to tell me this? "Well that's great," I said. "That's a really big honor. You shouldn't have been embarrassed to tell me that."

"Well, actually, there's more," she said.

"Yeah?"

"Well, there's this big school district awards banquet," she said. "It's one of those end-of-the-year things, where they give out all the student and teacher awards." She glanced up at me and then immediately looked down at the ground again. "The superintendent and the mayor and all kinds of people come to it," she said. "It's really fancy. I'm supposed to give an acceptance speech and everything."

"Cool," I said. "You deserve it."

"Well, my family gets four seats at the banquet," she said. "But as you know, there are only three of us."

I saw it coming now. I knew why she was so nervous. Maybe I could head it off before she popped the question. "So, I'll bet you're going to ask one of your friends from school," I said. "I'm sure any of them would love to go with you."

"Well that's the thing," she said. "I mean, I like the kids at school and all—but sometimes they act like 10-year-olds."

"Phoebe, they *are* 10-year-olds."

"I know," she said. "But this is a very fancy banquet. And all the teachers will be there. So I thought I might invite someone a little more—you know—mature. Maybe someone older than me."

I could feel the trap closing on me.

"So anyway," Phoebe said. "I was thinking—well, what I'm wondering is—" She couldn't get it out. She couldn't come right out and ask me.

Just then the smoke alarm went off again. "Oh, oh," I said, jumping at the opportunity. "Sounds like the fire's spreading. I'd better get back inside." I leaped up off the step and darted inside. "See you, Pheeb," I called back to her and swung the door shut behind me.

On the platter in the middle of the table was a stack of brownish flat things that looked like old leather moccasins in a steaming mud sauce. Mom, with a broad smile fixed on her face, picked up the platter and lifted one of them onto her plate with the serving fork. It occurred to me that Mom had never served herself first at the table before. But this wasn't a regular meal. Ordinary table manners didn't apply. By taking the first serving, Mom was actually trying to protect her family. If she took the first bite, we'd know if it was safe for the rest of us.

She passed the platter to Orville. He scrutinized its contents a few seconds—obviously looking for the smallest serving—and finally placed one on his plate with the fork. He handed the platter to me and then grimly looked down at his plate.

I looked the flat things over. I had no idea what they were. Amanda just sat looking down into her empty plate. I swallowed, stabbed one of the things with the fork, and put it on my plate. After I passed the platter on to Dad, I scraped off some of the brown sauce to see if I could identify what was underneath. I couldn't.

I glanced around the table. Dad was still trying to decide what to do with the platter of alleged food he was holding. The rest were looking down at their plates and fiddling with their silverware, stalling for time.

I cleared my throat. "Exactly what is this?" I asked. It seemed like a fair question to me, considering the circumstances.

Amanda looked about to cry. "*Mo-om,*" she said, never taking her eyes off her empty plate. "Make him stop."

"Honey, don't be rude," Mom told me. "It's obviously a pork chop."

That's all it took. Amanda instantly burst into tears. "It's chicken," she said. She jumped up from the table, making the plates and glasses jump, and stomped out of the room. I heard her footsteps bound up the stairs and thump across the ceiling as she made her angry way to her room.

The four of us sat in embarrassed silence. I could hear water dripping in the kitchen sink.

"Well, let's eat," Mom said.

We all just sat there.

"It sure smells good," Dad said. This from someone who breathes model glue fumes all day.

Mom cut a tiny corner off her piece of chicken and put it in her mouth. She made the face a baby would make if it bit into a lime. She delicately raised her napkin to her lips so she could discretely spit it out.

A minute later the four of us were in the kitchen while Dad made us all sandwiches. I tried to get Sadie, our cocker spaniel, to eat the chicken, which I'd cut up and piled into her bowl. She sniffed at it and picked up a piece in her mouth. She immediately dropped it again. I'd never seen a dog make a face before, but she made one then. She looked up at me as if I had somehow betrayed her, and then she bounded out through her doggy door with her stubby tail tucked between her legs.

Dad piled the sandwiches he'd just made on a plate and turned to carry them to the table. Before Dad had set the plate down, the phone rang. Mom picked it up.

"Oh, hi, Doris," she said into the phone. Doris was Phoebe's mom.

Dad went to one of the drawers for a knife to cut his sandwich in half. I picked up one of Dad's sandwiches and bit into it. I leaned over to Orville who was chewing hungrily. I know it was mean, but I whispered, "I'd rather eat anything, anywhere, with anyone, than eat something Amanda cooked."

Orville laughed through his mouthful of sandwich.

"Yes, of course," Mom said into the phone. "Willie would love to go to the banquet."

I suppose I deserved it.

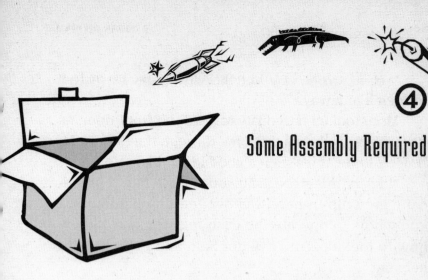

Some Assembly Required

Although no one ever actually said anything, it was clear we all agreed that Amanda should no longer do the cooking. After that, Mom started going home at five o'clock and leaving me at the shop to sweep up and wait for Dad. Sometimes Dad would get there first, and sometimes it was Orville, fresh from baseball practice. We'd help Dad do the books and lock everything up, and then we'd all head home. Most days, Sam and Felix came over to the shop after school, and they'd do their homework at the counter and help out when they could. We'd drop them at their houses on our way home for dinner.

"It's so quiet today," Mom said, one afternoon after she'd been running the shop a week or so. "Maybe it would be okay." She was considering leaving me and Sam and Felix in charge for the last hour of the business day so she could do some grocery shopping on her way home.

"We'll be fine," I told her. "We'll close up at five o'clock like always."

Mom looked nervously toward the front door, as if wondering who might come through the door next. "I don't know if it's such a good idea," she said.

"I know this store inside out," I told her. "I practically grew up in here. I've waited on customers. I know how to operate the cash register, and I know how to lock up. And I've got Sam and Felix here to help me."

Mom sighed. "It's a big responsibility," she said. "I'm not even sure if it's legal."

I looked at my wristwatch. "It'll only be an hour or so," I reminded her. "We'll be fine."

Mom sighed and bit her lower lip. "Okay," she said at last. "But be careful—and call me if you need anything."

"Okay," I said. "But we're not going to need anything."

Mom went out the front door. I watched her through the window as she crossed the street to her car. She opened the car door, but before she got inside, she glanced anxiously back at the store, like she was having second thoughts. I smiled and waved to her, trying to put her mind at ease by showing her how confident I was. She forced a smile, waved back, and got in her car.

When she pulled away from the curb, Sam and Felix were standing on either side of me, waving to her as well.

"Finally," Felix said, when Mom's car was out of sight. "This is our chance to run things right."

Both Sam and I turned to look at him.

"No offense," he said. "But your parents are lousy businessmen." He turned his back to the window and surveyed the store with his hands on his hips. "If this place was run right, you'd be a nationwide chain by now. You'd all be millionaires. You'd be the McDonald's of hobby shops."

"What do you mean, 'If this place was run right'?" I asked him. "My parents work hard to keep this place running."

Felix shook his head dismissively. "You've got to think big," he said. He spread his hands out in front of him. "National television ads, celebrity spokespersons, million-dollar giveaways."

"Well, we've got an hour before we close up," Sam teased. "Which of those things do we do first?"

"Let's do a million-dollar giveaway," I said. "I think I saw a million dollar bill in the cash register."

"Okay," Felix said. "You're both very funny, but there are some simple things we could do to increase profit around here."

"Like what?" I asked.

Felix thought about it a moment, rubbing his chin, his brow furrowed in thought. "Okay," he said. "Here's an idea—just off the top of my head."

Sam eyed him suspiciously. "We're all ears," she told him.

"In this busy world, people are always looking for ways to save time," Felix said. "On Freddie's last birthday, my dad bought him a bicycle. And he paid an extra $15 for one that was already assembled, so he wouldn't have to spend all that time doing it himself."

"Yeah," Sam said. "So?"

Felix waved his hand around in the air. "Well, practically everything we sell here requires assembly," Felix reasoned. He pointed to a shelf on our left. "I mean, just look at all these jigsaw puzzles."

"Brilliant," I said. "So you're saying that when someone buys a jigsaw puzzle, we offer to put it together for them, if they pay extra."

"Three dollars," Felix said. "That sounds fair. Unless it has really small pieces, then we'd have to—"

"Isn't putting it together the entire point?" Sam interrupted. "Why not just buy a picture?"

Felix thought it over. "Well maybe not the jigsaw puzzles," he said. "But what about all those models?"

Sam rolled her eyes. "You just don't get the whole hobby concept, do you?" she said.

Just then the bell over the door jingled and the three of us turned in unison to see our first customer—a little round man with a beard.

"Hi," the three of us said in eerie unison. "Can I help you find anything?"

The man took a step backward, as if he might just bolt for the door, and eyed us warily. "Models," he said. "World War II tanks."

"Right this way," I told him. I led him to the correct aisle, Felix and Sam on our heels. The three of us stood there watching him as he picked up a box and carefully read it. He kept glancing up at us, a look of edginess in his eyes.

"Thanks," he said. "I think I'll be okay now. You can all go back to what you were doing."

"Yes, Sir," we all said in unison again. He backed away another step, so we just left him alone. He was our first customer, and we didn't want to frighten him away.

I went behind the counter and stood by the cash register. Sam and Felix went over by the front window. They were talking to each other, but I couldn't hear what they were saying.

I glanced down at the wooden floor. The patch under my feet was worn down to white wood from all the years Dad had stood on this very spot, ringing up customers. I looked out at the store—aisle after aisle of hobby supplies, airplanes, and kites hanging from the ceiling.

This is what my dad saw, hour after hour, day after day. While I was out having fun with Felix and Sam, Dad was right here, earning the money that would buy the clothes I wore, the food I ate, the bike I rode. Just standing there made me feel grown up and responsible, like part of my life was ending and a new chapter was about to begin.

Sam and Felix came over from the window and stood on the other side of the counter. "The front window," Felix said. "That same train set has been there for years."

"So?" I asked.

"Well, that's the part of the shop the world sees," he said. "If you want to do better business, you should think about changing it every once in a while to get people's attention."

I looked over at the front window. The train ran along its miniature track, disappearing into the little tunnel and reappearing on the other side, as it had done millions of times before. The mountain that had once been a lush grassy green had faded in the sun, and the village of tiny houses lay under a gray film of dust. Maybe Felix had a point there. But before I could respond to him, the little round man brought a model tank up to the counter. I noticed that he stood a safe distance from where Felix and Sam were standing.

"Let me ring you up," I said. "Do you need any glue or paints today?"

"No thank you," he said.

I rang the price into the cash register.

Felix stepped up closer. "We'd be happy to assemble that model for you for a small fee," Felix told him.

The man didn't answer. He just looked at Felix and backed a few feet further along the counter. When I gave him his change and the model in a plastic bag, he practically ran out the door. The bell above the door jingled wildly behind him.

"I don't think we'll be seeing *that* customer again any time soon," Sam said.

He was our last customer that day. At five o'clock I locked the front door and turned the sign in the window to CLOSED. I went to the back room and got the broom so I could start sweeping up. When I came back out front, Felix was bent over the discount shelves rummaging through the odds and ends that had gathered there over the years.

Felix straightened up with a can of fluorescent green spray paint in one hand and a porcelain doll's head in the other. "Look at this," Felix said, a note of disbelief in his voice. "All this stuff is under-priced."

"That's because no one wants it," I said. "That stuff's been collecting dust for years." Sam came up and stood next to me.

"Yeah," Felix said. "But it's all priced below cost. You lose money every time someone buys something."

"Getting *any* money for this stuff is better than getting no money for it," Sam pointed out. "Nobody wants it."

"There's got to be someone out there in the world who wants it," Felix said. "There's got to be *someone* who would pay full price."

I picked up a reel of glow-in-the-dark kite string. "Sure," I said. "There might be someone out there who'd pay full price for this, but what are the chances he's going to wander in here any time soon?"

"eBay!" Felix said. "You can sell anything on eBay!"

I looked down at the roll of kite string in my hand and tried to imagine it. I shook my head. "By the time we paid for postage, we'd have lost all the profit anyway."

"The buyer pays for shipping and handling," Felix said triumphantly. "It wouldn't cost us a penny. It's pure profit."

Maybe I'm just old-fashioned, but it didn't sound like such a hot idea to me. "I don't know, Felix," I said. "What do you think, Sam?"

Sam shrugged. "If someone's stupid enough to bid on the world's largest egg timer, there just might be someone stupid enough to buy this stuff," Sam admitted.

"Listen to her," Felix said. "It's true."

I sighed. Over the years, I'd learned to be very skeptical about Felix's schemes. "I don't think Dad's going to go for it," I said.

"Come on," Felix begged. "I could sell every item on this table for 10 times what you're asking."

Sam grinned suddenly. "Then why not do it?" Sam asked. "Why not buy all this stuff from Willie and keep the profit yourself?"

I smiled. If I sold everything on the discount shelves in one afternoon, I'd be a family hero. "That sounds like a win-win proposition to me," I said.

Felix eyed the discount shelves more skeptically now. It would be *his* money on the line. He looked at Sam and then at me, as if he was trying desperately to come up with a satisfactory excuse.

"Come on, Felix," Sam said. "Put your money where your mouth is."

Felix ran a finger around the inside of his tee-shirt collar. "Okay," he said. "I will. Total it up, Willie. I'm taking all this stuff home."

That night on the way home, I got Dad to swing by the photo shop to pick up my last roll of film. I sat in the back seat of the car with Sam and Felix, and we passed the photos around. The one with our family outside Hobby City turned out well, but the best one was of me and Sam and Felix and Phoebe outside my house in the late afternoon sun. The four of us sat on the porch steps and smiled, sunny and carefree, while the sun lit up the lawn and the trees and the house behind us.

"I want a copy of this," Sam said, looking at the photo as we drove. "I don't think we've ever had a photo of all of us together."

"Here," I said. I pulled out the brown strips of negatives and held them up to the car window until I found the right one. "Just give it back when you're done with it."

Over the next week, Amanda seemed to grow more and more energetic. In her mind, she was already away at college, although she still had a few more weeks of high school to get through. She'd already mapped out the next four years and most of her career as a nurse beyond that. She bought a Midland University sweatshirt that she wore everywhere, though the thermometer was climbing toward summer. For all I knew, her bags were already packed and waiting on the floor of her closet.

But while Amanda was bursting with energy and enthusiasm, the rest of us had slowed to a crawl from sheer exhaustion. Dinner seemed to get later each night as Mom struggled to keep the store and the house both running smoothly. By the time I got home, and ate dinner, and did my homework, I could barely keep my eyes open. I actually fell asleep in Mr. Keefer's science class one morning, and woke up, thinking I was in my bedroom, to find Sam poking me from across the aisle with her pen.

"What's wrong?" she asked me.

"Nothing," I told her groggily. "I was just resting my eyes."

Dad had the worst of it. Each night he seemed to fall farther behind and to grow more anxious. He'd started leaving the house before dawn for the long commute to Cedarville—it was the only way he could spend enough time at the new store to keep it running and still make it back in time to have dinner with our family. He had dark lines under his eyes now, and he nodded off every night soon after dinner while he was sitting on the living room sofa.

Even Orville was tired. His grades, which were nothing to brag about in the first place, began to fall, and instead of starting as shortstop, he now rode the bench through the first innings, sometimes through the whole game.

If it wasn't for Amanda's enthusiastic monologues about Midland University each night at the dinner table, we'd probably all have eaten in silence and then shuffled away to sleep with the dishes still on the table.

"What's the camera for?" Amanda asked me cheerily one morning at the breakfast table.

It was just the two of us: Amanda and I. Dad had left the house hours ago, and Mom had stayed up late cleaning the kitchen so she was still asleep. Orville had already left for school so he could fit in a workout and try to get his starting position on the baseball

team back. My math book was open beside my plate.
I was trying desperately to finish the last few prob-
.lems I'd been too tired to solve last night. I was frustrated and tired. The last thing I wanted was to be
stranded at the breakfast table with my perky, soon-
to-be-college-student sister.

"Sam asked me to bring my camera so I could
help her take candid shots for the yearbook," I
informed her curtly. "But if you don't mind, I'd rather
not talk. I'm behind in my homework." I picked up my
pencil.

"*Man,*" Amanda said. "What's gotten into everybody these days? Everyone's so cranky."

"If you weren't so selfish, you'd *know* why everyone's so cranky," I snapped. I slapped my pencil down
on the table. "We're all killing ourselves trying to keep
both stores open." I slammed my math book shut,
even though I had two more problems to do. I leaned
across the table at Amanda. "Do you have any idea
how hard Mom and Dad are working?" I asked her.
"I'm starting to think we should give up the store in
Cedarville. It just isn't worth it."

Amanda looked stunned that I would say such a
thing. "But we've *got* to keep the store open," Amanda said. "This is the chance of a lifetime for me."

I wanted to throw my book at her. "Think of
someone else for a change," I told her. "Dad's made
sacrifices his whole life for us. Keeping these two

stores open is killing him. Sometimes we kids have to make sacrifices for the family too."

"But this is important to me," she said.

"I know," I said. "But just look at him. It's too much work."

Amanda looked down at her plate a long time. I thought she was sulking, but apparently she was thinking things over. After a few seconds, she raised her head and looked me in the eye.

"What if he closed the shop here in Glenfield?" she said. "The one in Cedarville makes much more money. We'd probably have enough then—and Dad wouldn't be running two stores."

I blinked twice. I'd just assumed that if we went back to having one store, it would be the one in Glenfield. "But he'd still be driving all that way every day," I objected.

"Not if we moved to Cedarville," she said.

It felt like a wall of the kitchen had fallen away in front of me. It was impossible. We'd lived here in Glenfield all my life. Everyone I knew and loved was here. We'd never leave.

"Out of the question," I said. "I don't want to leave Glenfield. This is where all my friends are."

Amanda sat back in her chair and folded her arms. She regarded me coolly. "Well, *now* look who's not willing to make sacrifices for the good of the family," she said.

That day, I left for school with my backpack on one shoulder and my camera hanging around my neck—but the weight on my shoulders seemed far greater.

Amanda was right. Moving to Cedarville would solve a lot of our problems. Mom and Dad wouldn't be working so hard, and Amanda could probably still go to college.

But it was impossible. We couldn't move away— *could we?*

As I trudged to school, I prayed that the same idea would never occur to Mom and Dad.

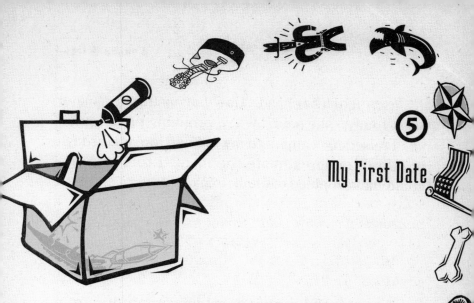

"I really appreciate this," Sam told me. "If you're taking pictures too, the yearbook'll be done in half the time."

We were in the back of Mr. Keefer's class first period, sitting in our usual seats. My camera sat on the desk in front of me.

Sam held up a brown paper bag and shook it before handing it to me. "There are 10 rolls of film in here," she informed me. "I've got another 10 rolls for my camera." She handed me the bag. "Try to use them all, but don't waste any shots," she said. "Our budget for the year is completely spent."

I opened the back of my camera while students were still filing into class. I loaded a roll of film and adjusted the settings. "Maybe I'll get lucky," I said. "Maybe I'll get a shot of one of Mr. Keefer's explosions. That's a daily part of Glenfield Middle School that's never been sufficiently documented."

Sam shook her head. "He's demonstrating a meter stick today," she said. "We're probably pretty safe."

I raised the camera to my eye and looked through it. "Don't underestimate the man," I told her. "He could make a piece of chalk explode."

It was weird carrying the camera around from class to class, snapping pictures everywhere I went.

Maybe it was my talk with Amanda that morning, but I began looking at things differently. There was so much about this place I'd want to remember if I ever had to move away. I wanted to remember how Coach Askew would sit us under the big schoolyard oak tree on hot days and tell us funny stories about his college football days when we should have been running laps. I wanted to remember Mr. Lander's loud checked suits. I wanted to remember how the hallways looked when they became rivers of students surging toward the doors after the final bell. I wanted to remember each of my friends.

And so I took pictures of all those things—winding shot after shot through my camera. A girl staggering under a stack of books in the library; a group of flag football players, spattered with mud, marching in from PE; a boy trying to shake a stuck candy bar from the vending machine—I took photos of everything.

As I did, I began to notice how beautiful the everyday things around me were. I noticed the way the light slanted in through the second story windows. I noticed the worn patches on the stairs from the thousands of students who had climbed them over the years. I noticed the young, promising faces all around me. I didn't want to leave any of this behind.

This was my history—and it was a lot of other people's history as well. Once, when I was in seventh grade, I checked out a school library book on Leonardo D'Vinci. As I was signing the card at the library counter, I noticed my father's name, Charles Plummet, near the top. He'd checked out this same book—printing his name in clumsy boyish letters—nearly 30 years before.

I wasn't just snapping pictures to help Sam out. I was helping preserve hundreds of memories.

I got to the cafeteria late for lunch—I'd stopped several times along the way to take photos. When I got there, Sam and Felix were already eating. I took my tray over and sat down with them.

"So how's the world of eBay?" I asked Felix when I was done saying grace. "Has anyone bid on that junk you took from the store?"

Felix began to fiddle with the things on his tray. "Sort of," he mumbled.

"Sort of?"

Sam elbowed him grinning. "Tell him," she said.

"It's still early," Felix said. "There's still a lot more time."

"Tell him," Sam said again. "Tell him about the one bid you got."

"You got a bid?" I said. "Well, that's not so bad, at least you can make some of your money back."

"Tell him," Sam said again.

Felix carefully aligned his knife so it was perfectly parallel to his fork. "I accidentally bid on it myself," he said.

"What?" I said. I burst out laughing.

"He had so many things listed, he forgot which ones were his," Sam explained. "And he ended up bidding on something he'd put up for sale himself the day before."

I laughed so hard my stomach began to ache. I had to lean on the table to catch my breath.

"A whole case of pipe cleaners for just $3," Felix said defensively. "It was such a great deal, I couldn't pass it up."

I shook my head. "If there are millions to be made on the Internet, I've got a feeling most of it is going to be made off Felix."

"Hey, laugh if you want," Felix said. He glanced down at his watch. "But in an hour and a half, someone at this table is going to be the proud owner of the world's biggest egg timer."

"I think that's just going to make us laugh harder," Sam pointed out.

Felix was more than an hour late in getting to the hobby shop that afternoon. Mom had already gone home—she'd been going home earlier and earlier, now that she trusted me with the store—and Sam and I had waited on a few customers on our own. I heard the bell above the door jingle, and looked up from behind the counter to see Felix shuffle through the door looking depressed.

"What's the matter with you?" I said. "You look like you got beat up."

He shuffled over and leaned against the counter, like he barely had the strength to stand. Sam came and stood next to him.

"What's the matter?" she asked. "Did something happen?"

He put his elbows on the counter. He ran his fingers through his hair and groaned.

I bent over the counter. "Felix, are you okay?"

"My bid won," he said. "I won the auction for the world's largest egg timer."

I stood up straight again. I was confused. "Well, isn't that *good* news?" I said. "Didn't you *want* to win?"

"I thought I did," he said.

"How much did you bid?"

"Nine dollars," he said. "And, unfortunately, no one went any higher."

"Nine dollars?" I said. "Sounds like a bargain to me."

"Nine dollars plus shipping and handling," he said. He lifted his head from his hands so he could look at me. "The thing's like six-feet-tall. It weighs 450 pounds," he said. "And because it's glass, they have to make a custom shipping container." He dropped his head back into his hands again. "And right now it's in Geelong, Australia."

"Australia?" Sam said. "How much is it going to cost to ship it over here?"

"In Australian dollars or American dollars?" Felix groaned.

"American."

He raised his head and looked up at the ceiling. "At this morning's exchange rate, it came to $647.50," he said. "And that's not counting my bid of $9."

I whistled. It was a lot of money. "Can't you just take back your bid?" I said. "Can't you tell them it was a mistake?"

Felix feebly shook his head. "It's all legally binding," he said. "And it was all in the fine print—I just didn't stop to read it. I was swept away in the excitement of the auction."

"Where are you going to get that kind of money?" I said.

"My dad's lending it to me, but I'm banned from computer use until I pay it all back," he said. He looked up suddenly. "Maybe I could sell the thing once it gets here," he said hopefully. "Maybe I could sell it for enough money to pay my dad back."

"Are you nuts?" I said. "Who's going to want a six-foot egg timer?"

Felix thought about it. "Maybe someone with bad eyesight who really likes soft-boiled eggs," he said. "Some old lady around here would probably love it."

"Yeah," Sam said. "Some old lady who can heft 450 pounds every morning."

Felix shrugged. "It could happen." He was grasping at straws.

"Look," I said. "Dad knows that you and Sam have been helping me out at the store. Let me talk to him. Maybe we can start paying you for your work. We're making a lot more money now that we have two stores."

He seemed to brighten up a little. "Really?" he said. "You think he'd pay us?"

"It's worth a try," I said. "I can ask him tonight at dinner." And then I remembered. I slapped my hand to my forehead and groaned.

"What's wrong?" Sam wanted to know.

"The *banquet,*" I groaned. "I'm supposed to go to some school banquet with Phoebe's family tonight." I moaned. "She got named Geek of the Year or something. I tried to get out of it, but her mom called my mom—you know how it goes."

"Life is so unfair," Felix said, still slumped against the counter.

I slumped against the other side of the counter. "It is," I said. "It sure is."

"Oh, give me strength," Sam said, and went back to straighten up some shelves.

When Orville got to the shop a little after six, he told us that Dad had gone straight home. There was something he had to talk to Mom about. We'd meet him there for dinner.

We closed out the cash register and totaled things up the best we could, and then Sam, Felix, and I squeezed into the cab of Orville's truck, and he drove us home. We dropped Sam off first and then went by Felix's house.

When Orville stopped the truck in front of Felix's house, Felix was in no rush to get out. Things would be awkward at the Patterson table tonight because of the eBay egg timer episode.

Felix roused himself and climbed out of the truck. "You'll ask him?"

"About maybe paying you and Sam?" I said. "Sure, I'll ask him as soon as I get home."

Felix nodded and turned to face his house. He looked so small as he shuffled across the lawn and up the front steps.

When we got home, Dad's car was already parked in the driveway. I headed inside to find him. He wasn't in the living room, and Mom wasn't in the kitchen. I was about to head upstairs when I heard their voices coming from the room Dad uses as an office. I was about to knock on the door when I noticed how strange their voices sounded. To be honest the sound of their voices scared me. I froze there, my fist in the air, ready to knock.

"Honey, he's young," Mom's voice said. "He'll adapt. He'll be okay."

"I know," Dad said. "But still, there's got to be some other way."

"He'll understand," Mom told him "It'll take him a while, but he'll understand. And the other two will be fine. Amanda will get to go to Midland. She's so look-ing forward to it."

Dad sighed wearily. "Let's just wait," he said. "Let's wait and pray for the Lord's guidance before we do anything drastic. And if it's going to happen, I want everyone to be on board."

I backed quietly away from the door. I didn't mean to eavesdrop. Honestly, I didn't.

I slipped up the stairs and lay on my bed looking at the ceiling. It was happening. Mom and Dad were talking about moving. My stomach churned. My eyes burned.

I just lay there, numb and stunned, as the room got gradually darker. I tried to pray. I tried to think about that Bible verse about bad things working out for good. But it just wouldn't come to me.

I almost forgot about Phoebe's banquet.

If Mom hadn't come and knocked on the door to see what I was wearing, I might have missed the banquet entirely.

"I know you're not very excited about this," Mom said. "But this is a big night for Phoebe." Mom went over and looked in my closet. She laid a nice shirt and a pair of nice pants across the foot of my bed. "I know you're tired, but try your best to be nice to Phoebe tonight," Mom said. "This evening will mean a lot to her."

I wanted to ask her why it would mean so much. Was it because she wouldn't always have me next door to have a crush on? Was it because we were moving to Cedarville once school let out? But I didn't ask. I just waited for Mom to leave the room and then I changed into the clothes she'd set out for me.

When I got downstairs, Mom had a little bouquet of white daisies for Phoebe. "I got them from the gro-

cery store," Mom told me. "Tell her they're from me
and that I'm very proud of her."

When I got over to Phoebe's house, she was wearing a white frilly dress she sometimes wore to
church—but what surprised me was that her parents
weren't dressed up at all. Her dad sat in a chair watching the news while her mom fluttered around Phoebe
like a moth around a porch light, making final adjust-
ments to her dress and her hair. I'd never seen Phoebe
so dressed up.

I looked down at what I was wearing—a nice
shirt and a pair of slacks. I was definitely under-
dressed compared to Phoebe. Her mom went over
and picked up a small camera on the entry table.

"Maybe I should go home and put on a tie," I said.

Phoebe's mom was fiddling with her camera now.
She looked me over. "Nonsense," she said. "You look
just fine, Willie."

Phoebe looked up at me with her big brown eyes.
She looked a little nervous. "Get the tie," she told me.

This was Phoebe's big night, and Mom had told
me to be nice to her. If she wanted a tie, I'd wear a tie.
"I'll be right back," I told Phoebe's mom and started
for the door.

"Wait a minute, Willie," her mom said. "Did I see
you with a camera the other day?"

I paused with my hand on the front door knob.
"Yes," I said. "Why?"

She held up her camera. "This thing isn't working," she said. "I don't know what's wrong with it. Do you think we could take a photo with your camera? You two look so cute tonight, I'd love to get a picture."

Sam had said not to waste film, but surely one photo wouldn't make much of a difference. "Sure thing," I told her. "I'll be back in a flash."

When I got back to Phoebe's house, the tie firmly knotted under my chin, Phoebe stood in the hallway, and her mom hovered at the foot of the stairs. I handed her my camera.

Phoebe's mom posed us in front of the stairway, and looked at us through the viewfinder. "Wait a minute," she said. She went over to the entry table and got Mom's bouquet of daisies. She handed them to Phoebe, straightened my tie and went back to look through the camera's viewfinder again. "You two look so cute all dressed up," she said. "Give me a big smile."

I did the best I could to smile.

"Scoot closer together," Phoebe's mom kept telling us, although—arms at our sides—we were pressed shoulder to shoulder. "Say cheese," she said. The camera flashed.

We were pulling away from the curb, Phoebe and I in the back seat of her mom's Saturn, when it occurred to me that Phoebe's father wasn't in the front seat next to her mom.

"What about your dad?" I asked Phoebe. "Isn't he coming with us?"

Phoebe looked like she might be getting carsick. "Do you think I should start out my speech with a joke?" she asked me, changing the subject.

When we arrived at the hotel where the banquet was held, Phoebe's mom pulled up in front and waited for us to get out. Then she waved to us, smiling broadly, and drove away. I stood there as teachers and librarians and school bus drivers passed by with their husbands or wives or girlfriends or boyfriends. Everyone was dressed up. Everyone was smiling. Phoebe gave me a little push toward the door of the hotel. "Aren't we going to wait for your mom?" I said. "Where did she go to park the car?

Phoebe swallowed. "That closing line of my speech," she said. "Do you think it's strong enough?"

"Phoebe, what's going on here?" I asked her. "Where did your mom go—and why isn't your dad here?"

Phoebe glanced down at her watch. "Well, it's actually a rather funny story," she told me. "You see I thought I got *four* seats at the banquet—but it turns out I only get two."

Coach Askew walked by with his wife and nodded to me as he passed. The two of them disappeared into the hotel. Phoebe took me by the arm and pulled me a few steps toward the door, but then I stopped dead in my tracks.

"Wait a minute," I said. "You mean your mom just left? She went home?"

"She'll be back to pick us up when it's over," Phoebe said. She pulled on my arm again. We took a few more steps toward the door. I stopped dead in my tracks again.

"Wait a minute," I said. "You mean you and I are here alone?"

"Yeah," Phoebe said. "Pretty much." She pulled me a few more steps toward the front door. Then another thought occurred to me. I stopped dead in my tracks again.

"Wait a minute," I said. "You mean I'm your *date?*"

Phoebe nervously glanced around at the people passing us and going into the hotel. I think she was afraid I was going to make a scene. "I hear they're serving shrimp," she said.

"I can't believe you didn't tell me it was a date," I said. "That's the kind of thing you're supposed to tell a person."

Mom laughed. "Oh, Honey, it wasn't a date," she said. "She just wanted you to be there for her big moment. It was important to her."

Phoebe's mom had just dropped me off at home after a long and uncomfortable evening. Mom and I sat on the living room sofa on either side of Dad. The TV was on, but Dad's head was tilted back on the top of the sofa. He was snoring loudly.

"It was totally embarrassing," I said. "All my teachers saw me. They think I've got a 10-year-old girlfriend."

"They think no such thing," Mom told me. "Don't exaggerate. They think you were being kind to a little girl—and that's exactly what you were doing."

"She kept trying to get people to notice us," I said. "She kept laughing like a horse at everything I said."

Mom laughed. "How was her speech?"

"I don't know," I said. "By that time I'd slid under the table from pure embarrassment."

Mom laughed again. "You did a good thing," Mom said. "She'll always remember tonight."

I thought of Mom and Dad talking in the office when I got home from the store. "Is there a reason she'll need to remember it?" I asked.

Mom's smile faded a second and then came back again full force. "I'm not sure what you're asking," she said.

I thought I might as well be direct. "Are you and Dad talking about moving us all to Cedarville?"

Mom looked at me a long time before she answered. Then she nodded. "We're talking about it, Honey," she said. "But that's *all* we're doing. You *know* we'd never do anything like that unless everyone agreed."

I looked at the TV. "But why are you even *talking* about it?"

"This is wearing your dad out," Mom said softly, as if she didn't want Dad to hear. "We can't keep going on like this."

"But I thought we were going to hire a manager at the new store," I said. "I thought Dad was going to get someone to run it for him."

"There just isn't enough money," Mom said. "We can't afford to hire someone full time just yet. We had to take out a loan to buy the business from Mr. Paulson."

"Can't we just let the store go?" I said. "Can't we sell the business to someone else and go back to the way things were before?"

Mom mulled it over. "We could do that," Mom said. "But would that be fair to Amanda? Would it be fair to you when it was time for you to go to college? And your dad will need to retire sometime—we've got to start putting some money away."

I looked at Dad. His mouth was slightly open and he snored loudly. I knew how exhausted he was these days. I felt an ache in my throat. "How about if the stores started making more money?" I said. "Could he hire someone to run the new store then?"

"I suppose," Mom said. "But it's not that easy."

"We could advertise," I said. "We could run some promotions." I was starting to sound like Felix. "There's got to be something we could do."

"Well, if you can think of something, please let us know."

I left Dad and Mom on the sofa and went upstairs to my room. It was hard to sleep, so I lay there looking around at my shelves, at my desk, at my window. I'd lived in this room for as long as I could remember, and I'd always assumed I'd never be leaving it—at least until I was ready.

I felt a lump in my throat. There had to be something we could do. There had to be some way to get Amanda to college without having to move to a whole other town. I closed my eyes and prayed that God would work it out so I could stay. I prayed that He'd fix it so Dad could make more money. I prayed that Amanda would change her mind about college. I prayed that He'd make it so things could be the way they were before.

I prayed that the Lord would let me have *my* way.

I read a chapter of the Bible—like I did every night before I went to sleep—and switched off my light. Just as I was drifting off to sleep, the idea came to me: I'd call Tri-County Advertising, the people who owned the Hobby City billboard along the highway, and see if we could change the sign. Thousands of cars passed that billboard each day. Maybe if we could fix up the sign a bit, and let people know we bought the store, we'd get more customers! I fell asleep wondering if God was already answering my prayers.

The next day things at the hobby shop were pretty quiet, so in the afternoon, when Mom left, I stood at the counter with a pad of paper doodling and trying to come up with an idea for the billboard. Sam had left a half-hour ago to walk down to the photo shop and pick up all the pictures we'd taken for the yearbook.

Felix came behind the counter and looked over my shoulder as I doodled. "What are you doing?" he wanted to know.

"Trying to think of a slogan," I told him. "I called about the billboard out on the highway, and the people who own it say we're all paid up for the year—we can change it every three months free of charge. Dad said I could try to think of what to put up there."

"This is perfect," Felix said, rubbing his hands together. "This is exactly the kind of marketing I was talking about. Let's get a celebrity spokesperson and plaster their face up there."

"All I'm trying to do is think of a slogan," I told him, feeling a little impatient. "I took a good shot of the new store with my camera. All of us are standing outside it. I just have to think of what to write underneath."

"But you can't write just *anything*," Felix insisted. "This is a big marketing opportunity. We've got to come up with a great slogan. That's the key."

"I'm just trying to—"

"But it's got to be catchy," Felix interrupted. He was off and running. "I bet I could come up with a hundred of them."

"I'd settle for one," I told him.

Felix's eyes darted around the store and came to rest on a shelf of new model airplane kits. "I've got it!" he said. He dashed over and grabbed one of the boxes and then held it out in front of him. "Just Glue It," he announced.

I sighed. "I think the Nike people might have a problem with that one," I pointed out.

"Right, right," Felix said. He set the model back on the shelf. "I thought it sounded familiar. But, hey, I'm just getting started here. How about 'Got Hobbies?'"

"We're not going to *steal* a slogan," I told Felix. "All we've got to do is let people know that our family has taken over Hobby City."

"How about '*Yo Quiero* Hobbies?'" Felix suggested.

"How about you go wait on that customer?" I told him.

Felix went over and said something to the woman who had just come in the store, and then he led her back to the section where we kept the remote control cars.

I wrote a sentence on my pad of paper: THE PLUMMET FAMILY PROUDLY PRESENTS ITS NEW ADDITION. It wasn't terribly catchy, but it would do.

The bell over the door jingled again. I looked up to see Sam come in carrying a bunch of photo envelopes. "You should see these," she said. "The ones you took are great. You're a natural photographer, Willie."

"Let's see them," I said.

She brought the envelopes over and set them on the counter in front of me. "Try to keep them in the same order," she said. "And don't mix up the envelopes, or we'll never find the right negatives."

I started flipping through the photos, envelope after envelope—all those smiling faces and familiar places. A lot of them had turned out well, if I do say so myself.

I was going through one of the stacks when I came across the photo of Phoebe and me. "I'll take this one," I said, a little embarrassed.

"I was wondering about that one," Sam said. "Was that the night you went to the banquet?"

"Yes," I said. "And if you don't mind, I'll take the negative as well. I don't want this photo ending up in our yearbook as a joke."

I took the brown strip of negative and slipped it, like a bookmark, between the pages of my pad of paper.

"Speaking of negatives," Sam said. "I got a copy of the photo you took of the four of us in front of your house. Let me give you back the negative."

"Good," I said. "I think you have the negative I need for the billboard."

"What billboard?"

"It's out on the highway," I told her. "I'm going to give them the photo of my family in front of the new store. This will be the headline." I turned the pad of paper so she could read it. "What do you think?"

"A little advertising never hurts," she told me. She sorted through her envelopes and handed me the one with the negative I needed.

I had just locked the door and turned the OPEN sign in the window to CLOSED when I heard the buzzer for the backdoor ring. I assumed it was a delivery—although deliveries usually came in the morning, and it was a few minutes after five now. I got the dolly from behind the counter and wheeled it to the back room. I opened the backdoor and found a man in a brown uniform with a clipboard.

"Delivery for Felix Patterson," the man said.

"Felix Patterson?" I said. "Are you sure?"

He flipped a page over on his clipboard and nodded. "Felix Patterson," he said. "It says so right here."

"Okay," I said. "Let me go get him."

I went back out to the store and found Felix sweeping the wooden floor with a broom. "There's someone at the backdoor," I said. "It's some kind of delivery for you."

Felix glanced nervously at the door to the back room. "Could you finish sweeping up, Willie?" he said. "I'll be back in a few minutes."

"Sure thing," I told him. When I was done sweeping, I went behind the counter to total up the cash register. Sam finished dusting the airplane shelves and came over to help me.

"It looks like we did pretty well tonight," Sam said.

"Yeah," I said. "That man who bought the train set really—"

I stopped in mid-sentence because of a weird rumbling noise. I felt the floorboards vibrate. At first I thought a big truck must be passing by outside, but I saw nothing through the front window except a few parked cars and a lady with a baby stroller.

"What in the world?" Sam said.

Felix came around the corner from the back room rolling some huge object covered by a blue paint-spattered tarp. He looked a little anxious, and more than a little strained by the effort. He parked the huge object in front of the counter and came out from behind it looking uneasy. He pulled the dolly to one side and pushed his glasses up on his nose.

Sam and I were speechless. We had no idea what was going on. We had no idea what to say.

"Behold!" Felix said. He grabbed a corner of the tarp and pulled it off.

There, parked in the middle of the floor, was a massive egg timer. My mouth fell open. It was like nothing I'd ever seen before. It was a huge red thing, shaped like an egg, with a gleaming hourglass in the middle. It was taller than Felix, taller than me even.

Like I said, it was shaped like an egg—but it was also shaped like a chicken, with two yellow chicken feet and a chicken head mounted on top. Stuck to it was a sign that said

BEHOLD!
THE WORLD'S
LARGEST
EGG TIMER!

I just stood there blinking. The world's largest egg timer was standing in the middle of my family's store. There was really nothing appropriate to say.

"You had it delivered *here?*" Sam sputtered. "What were you thinking?"

Felix forced a grin. "I was thinking it was exactly what we needed," Felix said. "It'll be great publicity."

Sam stepped closer to the giant egg timer and looked it up and down. "In other words, your mom said you couldn't take it home," Sam said.

Felix pushed his glasses higher on his nose again. "Well that entered into it," he admitted. "But believe me, people will come from all over to see the world's largest egg timer."

Sam shook her head. (I still hadn't regained the power of speech.) "Who in their right mind is going to want to see *that?*" Sam said. "And it couldn't be the world's largest hourglass. I've seen one much bigger than that."

"It's not the world's biggest *hourglass,*" Felix said like he was talking to a 4-year-old. "It's the world's biggest *egg timer.*"

"And the difference is?"

"It takes exactly three minutes for the sand to run through," Felix said proudly. He twisted a wheel on the side of the monstrous contraption, and the hourglass inside turned over. Sand spilled through the narrow middle. "Despite its size, this baby could time the perfect soft-boiled egg. It's a miracle of craftsmanship."

My mouth was moving by now, but no sound was coming out.

"And it's so practical," Sam said. "I'm surprised every kitchen doesn't have one."

"You can't just park it here," I finally sputtered. "We're trying to run a business."

"I know," Felix said. "That's why it's here. We'll put it in the front window instead of the moldy old train set. It'll be the biggest draw you've ever had."

I just stared at it and shook my head in wonder. My reflection was distorted in the curved glass. "You've got to get this out of here before my dad sees it," I begged him. "They'll never leave me alone in the store again."

"Come on, Dude," Felix said. "At least let your dad *see* it. What if he thinks it's a great idea?"

"Felix, get it out of here," I said. "Call back the guy with the clipboard."

"Okay, look," Felix said. "If your dad sees it and doesn't want it in the store, I'll get it out of here if I have to roll it all the way home on the dolly. But at least let him decide if he wants it."

I sighed. I didn't know how Dad would react. This wasn't a situation he'd encountered before. I had no idea what to tell Felix. I looked at Sam. She shrugged.

"You're the boss," she said.

I groaned and ran my fingers back through my hair. "Okay," I said. "I'll call my dad and ask him to come by on his way home. But if he doesn't want it, you've got to get it out of here tonight."

"Deal," Felix said. He looked instantly relieved. "But before you call your dad, can I use the phone?"

Dad just walked around the giant egg timer, his mouth hanging slightly open. Orville, who by coincidence had shown up at the same time, couldn't stop giggling.

"It came from where?" Dad asked.

"Geelong, Australia," I said.

"It's near Melbourne," Felix added, as if that might make a difference to my dad.

"And why is it here?"

"It's for the front window," Felix said. "It'll be good for business. People will stop to see the world's largest egg timer in the window—and then they'll come right in and buy a kite."

If there was a cause-and-effect relationship there, I didn't see it.

Dad didn't seem to either. He looked a little irritated, and he was shaking his head. But his mouth wasn't all the way closed yet, so I knew he was still processing the information. It was a lot to take in.

Just then we heard a knock on the front door of the shop.

Dad looked up at the door. "Who could that be? We closed an hour ago."

"It's probably Mr. Topper," Felix said.

"The newspaper editor?" I asked.

Felix nodded. "He's here to see the egg timer," Felix said. "When I talked to him on the phone, he was very interested. He said it might end up on the front page."

I went over to the front door, and sure enough, there was Mr. Topper, a camera hanging on a strap around his neck.

I stood back to let him in, and he made a beeline for the giant egg timer. For a while he just circled around it, rubbing his chin. No one said anything.

"This might actually end up on the front page?" my dad asked finally.

Mr. Topper shrugged. "It was a pretty slow news day," he admitted. "The front page is either this or the twins born over at the medical center." He lowered his voice confidentially. "And between you and me, they were pretty ugly babies."

Dad looked at Felix and then at Mr. Topper and then at the huge egg timer. "So if we put this in the front window," Dad said, trying to sort it all out in his head, "you'll take a photo, and our hobby shop will be on the front page?"

Mr. Topper nodded. "The front page is all yours," he said. He glanced down at his wristwatch. "Unless some cuter twins are born between now and 10 o'clock."

So that's how it happened. Between Dad and Orville and Mr. Topper (the rest of us just got in the way when we tried to help), it took 15 minutes to lift the world's largest egg timer into place in the front window.

When it was safely on display, we turned on every light in the store, and all of us went outside (Dad was holding his lower back by now) while Mr. Topper took a few shots of the front window for the *Glenfield Gazette*.

The article that ran under the photo the next morning told the whole story of how Felix bought the egg timer on the Internet and how it had been shipped from Geelong, Australia, at considerable expense.

The weird thing was, it actually worked. The next day when I showed up for work, there were six or seven people standing around the front window staring reverently at the huge red monstrosity.

Felix, Sam, and I had more sales that night than on any night we'd ever worked—though we didn't sell a single kite.

Friday afternoon, I headed over to Tri-County Advertising on my bike. It was a little bit weird. I was in a rush because I needed to get to the hobby shop to take over for Mom, so I rode straight and hard, pausing only for stoplights. It was so unlike me. I didn't jump off the curbs or stop at the comic book store or take the long way so I could ride through the park and come down the big hill on Taylor Street. I had responsibilities to take care of. I had a lot resting on my shoulders. I wasn't such a kid anymore.

I'd begun to notice a change in my parents too. They didn't tell me what to do so much these days. Dad didn't keep asking me if I was done with my homework and Mom didn't keep reminding me to eat right or to wear a jacket. They asked my opinion more and depended on me more. It was almost like we were becoming a household of equals—Mom and Dad and the three of us kids.

I'd been given a lot of adult responsibilities—and as a result, I wasn't acting so much like a kid.

I was about a block from Tri-County Advertising, about to cross an intersection, when a white minivan ran a stop sign and pulled right in front of me. I slammed on my brakes and lay my bike down in a skid to avoid being hit. The driver of the van didn't even stop to see if I was okay. From where I lay on the ground, I saw the van turn a corner and disappear. I stood up and pulled my bike up on the curb. My open backpack was still on my shoulders, but all of my books and papers were strewn on the ground. I picked them up, stuffed them all back in my backpack, and dusted myself off. My heart was pounding. My knees were shaking. I sent up a one-word prayer to God—THANKS!

When I got to Tri-County Advertising, I had just enough time to run in the door and leave everything for the new billboard with the receptionist. I tore open my backpack and found the form I'd filled out with the billboard slogan. "This is for the Plummet billboard," I told the receptionist. "I talked to Mr. Banks on the phone. He'll know what it's about. It's supposed to go up this weekend."

I gave it to her and then dove in my backpack again to look for the strip of negatives. It took me a few minutes, but I found the brown slip of film and set it on the receptionist's desk. "It's photo number four," I told the receptionist. "It's all explained on the form."

I dashed back out the door to my waiting bike before she could even answer, and pedaled as fast as I could to work.

The mail came late to the hobby shop on Wednesday, or maybe Mom left for home early, I don't know which, but I was at the hobby shop behind the counter when the letter carrier came in, nodded hello, and set the mail down on the counter. I told her thank you as she headed back out the door.

I wasn't really sure what to do with the mail. Sam and Felix were sitting on stools at the far end of the counter, silently doing their homework, so I flipped through the mail, looking at all the envelopes. They all looked very official—even the one that was addressed to Felix.

Felix?

I flipped back to that envelope, and sure enough, it was addressed to Mr. Felix Patterson, c/o Plummet Hobbies.

I set the other mail on the counter and looked closely at the envelope. The return address read:

The Offices of
K.B. Langly, Mayor
Moss Landing, Ohio

Puzzled, I carried the letter down to where Felix was working on his math. "First you got that egg timer delivered here," I told him. "And now you're getting your mail here. Your folks haven't thrown you out of the house, have they?"

Felix looked up from his math book. I held the envelope out with both hands so he could read it. He looked bewildered. He closed his math book and took the envelope. He read the envelope and pushed his glasses higher on his nose.

"What is this?" he asked.

"How should I know?"

He took the envelope and tore it open. He pulled out a letter on official-looking stationery and shook it open. As he did, a newspaper clipping fell to the floor. It was the front-page story about Felix and the world's largest egg timer.

I bent and picked up the clipping while Felix read the letter. I watched his eyes dart back and forth across the page. As they did, a look of concern came over his face.

"Is everything okay?" I asked.

Sam got up from her stool and looked over his shoulder. All I could see from where I was standing was a bunch of signatures at the bottom.

Felix kept reading. When he lowered the letter, he looked like he'd seen a ghost.

"I'm being sued," he said, "by the town of Moss Landing, Ohio."

"Sued?" Sam said. "Why are they suing you?"

"It says here that Moss Landing is home of the world's largest egg timer," he said. "It has something to do with the Annual Moss Landing Egg Festival. It's signed by the mayor, the entire city council, and some girl who was recently crowned Egg Queen."

He handed me the letter and I skimmed through it. It was full of legal jargon, so it was hard to follow what it was saying. "From what I can tell, they're suing you for damages," I said. "They're sending someone out here to take a deposition—whatever that is. It sounds serious."

Felix's eyes were wide now. He glanced over at the huge egg timer in the front window.

"Maybe we'd better get that thing out of the window," I suggested.

"We just have to take down the sign that says it's the world's biggest egg timer," Sam said. "That's what all this is about."

It made sense, and it was certainly easier than moving the egg timer. I went to the front window, took down the sign, and slipped it behind the counter where no one could see it.

When I got back to the others, Felix was sitting on the stool, thumping his head on the counter.

"It's going to be okay," Sam told him. "Once they find out you're a kid, they won't really sue you. They'll just have the newspaper print a retraction or something like that."

"I'm in big trouble," Felix said, thumping his head every few words. "I'm going to end up in jail."

"Don't worry," I told him. "You can probably buy a good file from eBay and have it delivered to your cell."

Felix slowly raised his head and looked at me as if he couldn't believe what he'd just heard. It might have been insensitive, but at least he stopped thumping his head.

That night I was in the middle of a complicated algebra problem when I heard Mom call us down to dinner.

When I finally got to the dinner table, everyone was already seated. I pulled out my chair and sat down so Dad could say grace. Mom passed me the platter of chicken without asking what I'd been doing or why I was late. It was like she trusted me more now. It was like I was grown up and she didn't have to hear my excuses.

"So when *are* we going to talk about it?" Amanda said. I'd obviously entered in the middle of a conversation. "I'm graduating from high school in two weeks. I need to know what's going to happen to me next August."

"When are we going to talk about what?" I asked, putting a piece of chicken on my plate.

"Moving," she said bluntly. "Shutting down the Glenfield store and moving to Cedarville."

I set down the platter and glanced at Dad. He was looking down at his plate. I looked at Mom; she looked worried for me. I pushed my plate away. Suddenly I'd lost my appetite. "We're not really going to move, are we?" I said to the table in general. "We can't *do* that."

"And we *won't* do that unless everyone agrees that it's what the family should do," Dad said. He was looking directly at Amanda now. He sounded firm, which made me feel a little better. If it required a unanimous vote, it would never happen—because I would never vote for it.

"Well, *I* say we do it," Amanda said. "It makes sense all around. It's what's best for everyone."

"It's not best for *me*," I objected. "I don't want to move. I don't want to leave my friends."

"Don't be so selfish," Amanda told me, scowling. "Think of someone else for a change. Think of what's best for the whole family."

"*You* stop being selfish," I said. "You want to uproot the whole family just so you can go off to college. How is *that* thinking about other people?"

"Now, now," Mom said. "This is supposed to be a discussion, not an argument."

"I just don't want to move," I said. "This is our home. This is our town. We belong here. Everything was fine until we got the new store. We were all happy." I felt a lump growing in my throat. I thought of all the things I liked about living here. Everything was familiar. I knew everybody. If I didn't live in Glenfield, I wouldn't have my best friends, or my youth group at church, or even Phoebe.

"I don't want to move either," Orville said suddenly. "I think we should stay right here."

A wave of relief swept over me; at least I wasn't alone.

"You're going to be graduating next year," Amanda said, like she couldn't believe what she was hearing. "What's going to happen when you're ready to go to college?"

Orville shrugged. "Maybe I'll go," he said. "And maybe I won't. Maybe I'll get a baseball scholarship. It's not that important to me."

"Well, it's important to *me*," Amanda said, standing up angrily. "I want to go to college. I want to have a future. And you all want to take it from me."

Amanda stormed from the room. We all sat in silence listening to her footsteps stomp up the stairs and across the ceiling to her room. We heard her door slam, and then slowly, silently we ate our dinner.

I'd been planning to tell Dad about Felix's letter from Moss Landing, Ohio—but this just didn't seem like the right time.

On Saturday, Dad needed to put in some time at the Glenfield store, so he asked Orville to drive to Cedarville and run the new shop for the day. I asked Orville if I could go with him and help out. Tri-County Advertising had said they would try to get the new billboard up sometime this weekend.

We'd been on the road about a half-hour when we passed the billboard on the far side of the road. A white pickup truck was parked beneath the sign, and two men in white coveralls were looking up at it. One of them was pointing.

"That's *them*," I told Orville, excitedly. "By the time we come home, it should be done. We'll have our own billboard."

Orville just nodded.

Things were busy at the Cedarville shop. There was just so much more to keep track of there and so much more floor space to cover. At the end of the day, I was exhausted. My feet hurt and my shoulders were tight with stress. This, I knew, was how Dad felt every night when he closed up the shop.

We climbed into Orville's truck and headed for home, tired and looking forward to tomorrow's day of rest.

Although I was looking for the new billboard as we drove along that stretch of road, we were about 30 yards from it before I noticed it. Let's just say it wasn't at all what I was expecting.

"I don't believe it," Orville said. He hit the brakes and coasted over to the side of the road. He leaned over the steering wheel and peered up at the sign. He started laughing. "How did you manage *that?*" he asked.

I opened the door of Orville's truck and stepped out onto the weeds and gravel on the shoulder of the highway. My knees felt a little weak. I shielded my eyes with my hand and looked up at the giant, freshly painted billboard. The caption across the bottom was exactly the way I'd written it.

It was the picture that was the problem.

Instead of the photo of the Cedarville store, with the five of us standing in front of it, it was a giant photo of Phoebe and me before the school awards banquet. I just stared up at it feeling suddenly queasy. There it was, a hundred times larger than life— Phoebe in her white dress, holding a bouquet of flowers and looking up adoringly at me.

"The Plummet family is proud to present its new addition," Orville read aloud. I felt like I was slowly sinking into the ground. It was hard to think of a worse headline for that picture.

Orville laughed. "Wow," he said. "A new store and a new sister-in-law all in the same month. Things are moving pretty fast."

"Shut up," I told him.

I tried to piece together what had happened. Sam had given me back the negative I needed for the billboard, but I'd somehow mixed it up with the other strip of negatives—probably when everything spilled out of my backpack.

I'd given Tri-County Advertising the wrong negative!

A car full of teenagers passed by, but there was no way to block their view of the billboard. I just crouched down on the far side of Orville's truck, hoping none of them would see me. Thousands of people a day would see this billboard, I had thought the first time I saw the sign. It had sounded so good at the time.

"The soonest they can get to it is two weeks from Monday," Dad informed me once he'd hung up the phone. "Until then we'll just have to leave it the way it is."

"Can't I climb up there with a can of white paint and a roller?" I asked.

"Only the advertising company is allowed to paint up there," Dad said. "It would be trespassing. There's no way we can change it until they do it themselves."

I groaned.

"Look on the bright side," Orville said. "Maybe the two of you will get some nice presents."

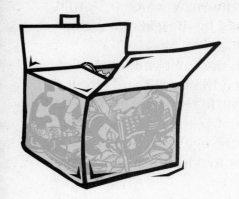

The man who showed up at the hobby shop on Tuesday afternoon was actually quite nice, and he wasn't from Moss Landing, Ohio—he was from just over in Pepperville. He wore a gray suit and carried a brief case. He told us that the town of Moss Landing had hired him to come out and talk to us and to photograph and measure the egg timer in question. He assured Felix that everything would be okay. Moss Landing was just trying to protect its claim as home of the world's largest egg timer. It meant a lot to them.

"Shouldn't we call your dad and tell him the guy's here?" Sam asked me when Felix took the man over to look at the egg timer.

"Well, actually, I haven't told Dad about the Moss Landing lawsuit yet," I admitted.

"What?!" Sam said. "How could you not tell him something like that?"

"I've been waiting for the right moment," I told her. "And there haven't been a lot of right moments in the last few weeks."

The man climbed up in the front window with a tape measure and measured the height and circumference of Felix's egg timer. He recorded everything in a black leather notebook. He took out a Polaroid camera and photographed the egg timer from behind and then again from outside, looking through the window.

Sam and I watched from inside the store as Felix walked the man to his car, which was parked right in front of the store. The man talked to Felix a few minutes and then shook his hand, got in the car, and drove away.

The bell over the door jingled when Felix came back inside.

"So?" Sam said. "What did he say?"

Felix paused and let the door swing shut behind him. "He said he hoped this would be the last I ever hear from Moss Landing," Felix said. "But there's no way to know what will happen next."

I was determined to tell Dad about the Moss Landing lawsuit that night at dinner. He looked tired and worn sitting at the table, but I knew I'd have to let him know—even though it was clear he didn't need another thing to worry about. Orville had a game that day—the last game of the year—so we started dinner without him.

Mom tried to be cheerful and to keep the conversation going, but no one wanted to cooperate. Dad was too exhausted to talk much. There were dark lines under his eyes, and—was it my imagination?—his hair looked grayer at the temples.

Amanda wasn't talking either. She was still angry that Orville and I weren't willing to move. She'd spent the last week glaring at me each time we passed in the hallway.

"So," Mom said, still trying to get some cheerful conversation going. "Did anything interesting happen at the store after I left?"

This was my moment. This was my chance to tell Dad what had happened with the egg timer. In my mind I tried to think of the best way to begin—a way that might make it all seem funny, and not the calamity it actually was. "Actually something interesting *did* happen," I volunteered. I looked at Dad. He was half listening. "We had a visitor who came to the store to—"

Just then the front door opened and Orville burst into the house. He grinned and dropped his bag of baseball equipment with a clatter on the floor. He looked flushed with excitement.

"Wow," Mom said. "I guess I know whose team won today."

Orville laughed. "You'd be surprised," he said. "I got to play three innings today, and we lost 14 to 3. It was great. I played really hard."

I grinned. "Not hard enough, apparently," I pointed out.

Orville just smiled. He came over to the table, turned his chair around, and straddled it backward. "We played Cedarville High," he said. "They're a great team. Half the guys are getting recruited by colleges. One of them is even going to the minor leagues when he graduates."

"I still don't get why you're so excited," Mom said.

"Well, I talked to their coach after the game," Orville said. "I told him we might be moving out his way. He said he needed a shortstop next year. He said he liked my hustle. He said if we move there, I can probably be a starter on his team."

My smile disappeared. "What?" I said.

"I'd like to change my vote," Orville said. "I'm thinking that moving to Cedarville is a pretty good idea."

Up in my room that night, I just lay on the bed feeling sorry for myself. I don't think I'd ever felt so alone.

Dad had said we wouldn't move unless everyone agreed—but how could we *not* move, when the only one who was against it was the youngest kid in the family?

Could I really hold out? If we stayed in Glenfield, Dad and Mom would have to give up the new store and make do with the business at Glenfield. They'd never be able to afford a decent vacation, let alone a good retirement. Amanda would glare at me every time I passed her in the hall. She'd sit through every meal, knowing that I'd kept her out of Midland University.

And now there was Orville. Sports were about the only thing he was really good at, and baseball was his favorite sport of all. If we stayed in Glenfield, he'd be sitting on the bench his senior year, on a team that wasn't very good. But if we moved, he could be the starter on the best team in the league. It could open doors for him. It could send him to college. It was something he really wanted.

But what about what I wanted? Didn't that count for anything? Did everyone expect me to just leave all this behind?

I rolled over on the bed and turned on my bedside light. I opened the Bible to tonight's chapter: Philippians 2.

I had just begun to read when I came to a verse I knew well. "Do nothing out of selfish ambition or vain conceit, but in humility consider others better than yourselves. Each of you should look not only to your own interests, but also to the interests of others."

I sighed and chewed on my lower lip. I knew that God was speaking to me through His Word. But that wasn't the message I wanted to hear right now.

The next week, the last week of school, another letter was delivered to the hobby shop for Felix. It was from Moss Landing, Ohio. Felix looked down at the second letter and then up at me. He clearly didn't want to open it.

"Go ahead," I urged him. "You've got to open it sometime. It might be good news."

"Good news," Felix said skeptically. "Right." He swallowed hard and tore open the envelope. His eyes darted back and forth over the page, and a bewildered look spread across his face. He peeked in the envelope and pulled out a second slip of paper and looked it over.

"So what does it say?" I asked him. "What happened?"

He looked up at me a little dazed and then looked at the letter again. "It says that my egg timer beat their egg timer by three-and-a-half inches," he said. "It *is* the world's largest."

"Really?"

He nodded at me, blinking and confused—as if a flash bulb had just gone off unexpectedly. "And by endorsing this check for $2000, I agree to destroy my egg timer and relinquish all claim to the world's record," he said.

He held the check up for me to read. I just stared at all those zeros and started to laugh. Only Felix could have managed to make a profit with a giant egg timer.

"I think I want to go home now," he said, drifting, still in a daze, toward the door.

"Take the afternoon off," I told him.

The bell over the door jingled and Felix was gone.

Wednesday that week, the yearbooks came out. They looked great, and we all carried them from class to class the last few days of school, passing them around and autographing them. We didn't do much of anything in our classes—the teachers were looking forward to summer as much as the kids.

On Friday afternoon the final bell rang, and school was over for the year. I walked down the front steps, swept along by a river of jubilant kids who were looking forward to a summer of freedom and fun.

I envied them.

Sunday afternoon after church, Sam, Felix, and I rode in Dad's car to the dump. The three of us sat in the back seat while Dad drove. Up ahead of us, the giant egg timer was tied down securely in the back of Orville's pickup.

At the dump, Orville backed his truck as far as it would go, and I opened the tailgate. It was easier moving the egg timer now, since it didn't matter if it got damaged. But even so, it took us nearly half an hour to roll it off the truck onto the ground, where it landed upright on its two chicken feet.

It was a windy, damp day, and the egg timer stood there amid the piles of trash and junk—looking for all the world like some UFO that had just arrived from a planet inhabited by giant poultry.

Dad draped a big blue tarp over it and went back to the truck for his sledgehammer. Felix and Sam and I stood next to one another looking at the tarp. And like a cold gust of wind, the realization came over me: this might be one of the last things the three of us would do together.

Dad brought the sledgehammer over and took up his position next to the egg timer.

"Whoever thought Dad would smash a world's record?" Orville quipped and then laughed at his own joke.

Dad swung the heavy hammer back.

"Wait," I blurted out. "Wait." I held my hand out to stop Dad's swing.

Dad set the hammer down with a thump and looked at me, puzzled. He clutched his lower back.

I wasn't sure why I'd stopped him. I tried to think of something to say. "We're about to smash the world's largest egg timer," I said. "How about we give it one last run? It seems only fitting."

Dad looked over at Orville and shrugged.

"Felix, why don't you do the honors," I said.

Felix stepped smartly up to the egg timer and pulled the tarp off. He looked so serious and stiff, I half expected him to salute it. He grabbed the knob on the side like a steering wheel and twisted. The hourglass inside somersaulted. Felix stepped back, and the five of us watched the sand slowly slip through the hourglass's waist.

For exactly three minutes we all stood there watching reverently. I felt Sam and Felix standing on either side of me, my two best friends in the world, and tried to cherish every last grain that fell. It was like the sands of time were slipping through my fingers.

That night I lay on my bed after everyone was asleep and flipped through my yearbook—page after page of faces I knew. Mixed in with the rows of student photos were all the candid shots Sam and I had taken. I knew each hallway and room in those photos. I recognized every drinking fountain, doorway, and backstop. I knew that school as well as I knew my house. Was it really possible I'd have to leave them both?

I looked inside the back cover at all the signatures and read the messages my friends had written. "See you next year," a lot of the messages said. But what if I never saw them again?

I knew what I needed to do, but I didn't want to do it. I closed my yearbook and opened my Bible. I was planning to read Philippians 3, but as I read, my eyes kept drifting back to words in the chapter before: "In humility consider others better than yourselves. Each of you should look not only to your own interests, but also to the interests of others."

It was hard guidance to follow. I wanted what I wanted—although I knew that was selfish.

For weeks I'd felt like I was growing up, like I was becoming an adult. But now I realized that I wasn't even close. I had more responsibilities now; that was true. But I was still thinking like a child.

I thought about Dad, how he made sacrifices every day for me—how he was killing himself trying to run two stores, just because I didn't want to move. I thought about Mom and how hard she had always worked for her family. Neither Mom or Dad put their own desires or interests first. They were real adults. They were living examples of God's selfless love for us. After all, God had give up a lot for me—His own Son.

I closed my Bible and switched off the light. I lay in the dark, listening to the house creak and wishing I could be a kid forever.

Sam and I stood behind the counter at the hobby shop on Monday afternoon. It was raining outside—a storm none of the weathermen on TV had predicted—and the shop was dark and cold and gloomy. We hadn't had a single customer all afternoon. In fact it was so slow that Felix had gone home to check on his eBay auctions, now that he had bought back his computer privileges.

Sam and I just stood behind the counter talking most of the afternoon. Before long it turned into a pretty serious talk, and our voices were soft in the empty dark store.

"I don't know what I should do," I told her. I had my elbows propped on the old wooden counter and had my head cradled in my palms. "Actually, I think I *do* know what I should do—I just don't want to do it."

Sam was oddly silent. Usually she was the one who gave me good advice. She was the friend I confided in, but this afternoon she hardly said a word.

"I mean it's really important to Amanda to go to college," I said. "And she actually got accepted at Midland." I listened to the steady hiss of rain on the high roof. "But Dad said we'd only move to Cedarville if it's what everyone wanted—and *I* sure don't want it."

I looked over at Sam. She stood at the tall front window, next to where the huge egg timer had stood, and looked out at the rain falling on Main Street.

"But if I make everyone stay here in Glenfield, Dad will have to give up the Cedarville store," I said. "That store does a great business and Dad could really use the money—there's college and retirement and all kinds of money things to think about."

I sighed and looked around at the dimly lit store. It looked worn and threadbare, but it was still a nice store by Glenfield standards. Why couldn't *this* place be a big money maker? Why couldn't *this* store bring in the customers like the place in Cedarville? I sighed.

The rain hissed on the roof high above us.

"I don't want to move," I said. "And I feel guilty for not wanting what everyone else wants. I feel like I'm holding the family hostage."

I looked over at Sam again. She was still silently looking out the window.

"Come on, Sam," I said. "Help me out here. This is really hard for me. Aren't you going to say anything?"

Sam turned slowly and faced me. Her eyes were rimmed in red and her cheeks were wet. She looked away for a minute, and then looked back at me. "This is really hard for me, too," she said.

For a while I just stood there looking at Sam's teary face and the gloomy rain running down the window behind her. I thought of all the things I should say. Things my mom and dad had already told me. "God takes care of us no matter where we go." "We'll always be friends." "The Lord is my Shepherd, I shall not want." But the words just wouldn't come. All I could do was look at Sam's tears and try to hold back my own.

I guess that's when I knew it. I guess that's when I knew I'd have to tell the others that I was willing to move to Cedarville. Sam knew it, and it was time I admitted it to myself: I had to do what was best for my family. I had to grow up.

Sam turned away from me and walked over to the window. She stood there looking out at the rain, her shoulders shaking with sobs. I went and stood beside her and put my arm on her shoulder. She leaned against me.

We stood there a few silent minutes, both looking out the window. A car passed by with its headlights on, and the cold gray rain fell everywhere. The windows of the shops across the street glowed behind the curtains of rain that fell from the window awnings. It really was a beautiful street—a beautiful town.

I would miss it.

I bent forward into the empty window display where Felix's egg timer had stood a few days ago. I looked as far as I could down this familiar street and knew the sands of time were quickly running out.

That night at dinner I told them. No one said anything after that. We all ate silently, looking down at our food.

A few days later, I was lying in bed half asleep when I heard the hammering. I sat up and looked at my alarm clock. It was 6:27 in the morning. I heard a car door slam and an engine start up. I went to the window just in time to see a gray Mercedes pull away from the curb and disappear down the street.

And there below my window, jutting up from the middle of the front lawn like a dagger, was a big white FOR SALE sign.

I went back and lay on the bed, but I knew I'd never get back to sleep.

My alarm clock went off at five o'clock, and I opened my eyes in a dark room. I sat up on the air mattress in my sleeping bag and looked around at the bare gray walls. For a second or two I wondered where I was, and then the sinking realization set in— this was the last time I'd ever wake up in this room. I reached over and shut off the alarm on the floor beside me.

I heard someone moving around downstairs. The sounds seemed oddly amplified and full of echoes in a house now empty of furniture. It was just Dad and Orville and me in the house now. We'd helped the movers all day yesterday, and we'd kept behind just what we needed to get through our last night in the house. Mom and Amanda were at the new house in Cedarville. When we got there later this morning, we'd begin unpacking all the boxes and trying to make the new house livable.

I got up and brushed my teeth and washed up without turning on the lights. I could hear Dad and Orville loading the last few things on Orville's truck, and then it was time to go.

I stood in the hallway and looked back through the dark doorway one last time at the room I will always remember. The shelves were empty. There were no posters on the wall, no bed, no desk. It was just an empty shell—and at that moment I felt like an empty shell too.

When I came downstairs, Dad and Orville were packing a box of cleaning supplies in the empty kitchen.

"We'll be right out," Dad told me. "Why don't you go on ahead?"

When I opened the front door, the sun was just beginning to light up the eastern sky. As soon as I stepped outside, I heard a tiny shivering cheer. There, huddled on the dark front lawn, were Sam and Felix and Phoebe. Sam and Felix held a poster-sized photo of the four of us sitting on the porch, our arms draped over each others' shoulders grinning into the sunlight of an afternoon that seemed so long ago. Phoebe had made a sign on poster board that said WE LOVE YOU, WILLIE.

I came down the front steps, blinking back the tears, and went to them, praying I wouldn't start blubbering. It was hard to look at my friends, so instead I inspected the poster they'd made. It was the photo I'd taken the day we'd come home from visiting Hobby City for the first time. There I was, surrounded by my friends, smiling a big, carefree grin. Would I ever feel that way again?

I forced myself to look at my friends' real faces. They were all sleepy, but they did their best to smile for me, although Phoebe already had tears running down her cheeks.

"We wanted to be sure you wouldn't forget us," Felix said. As if that would be a possibility. "We thought you might like to hang it up in your new room."

Behind me I heard a noise on the front porch. I knew that Orville and Dad had come out the front door by now, and that they were waiting on the front porch for me to finish my good-byes. I knew they were watching, but I didn't care.

Sam rolled up the poster. Felix stepped up and we started one of those casual back-slapping hugs that boys do to each other, but it suddenly became a real hug, and I squeezed him hard, knowing we'd never be this close again. When I let go of him and he stepped back, he was blinking, and he looked down at the ground with his hands dangling at his sides.

Sam handed Felix the rolled poster and then she stepped up to me with her arms open. I hugged her for a long time, and her face against my neck grew damp. I could feel her heart beating. Or was it my own?

When we let go of each other, she stepped back and smiled at me, even though her face was slick with tears.

Phoebe had set the sign she'd made on the lawn, and she practically ran up and tackled me around the waist. She hugged me more tightly than I thought possible, and I stroked the back of her head as her body shook with sobs. I thought she'd never let go of me—and, surprisingly, I wasn't sure I wanted her to.

When she finally let go, Felix handed me the poster.

"I get the sign too, don't I?" I asked.

Phoebe grinned through her tears and fetched the sign she'd made. She wiped off the dew with the sleeve of her sweater and handed the sign to me.

"It's a message I want to remember," I told her.

She grinned and hugged herself to stay warm.

For a few awkward seconds we all just stood staring at each other, and then my father cleared his throat behind me.

Felix sniffled. "It's only an hour away," he said. "We'll still see each other a lot."

I nodded. "We'll invite you all up for the weekend once we get settled in," I told them.

"Me too?" Phoebe wanted to know.

"Of course, you too," I said.

"And we can write and talk on the phone," Sam pointed out.

"Of course," I said.

And it was all true—but still, things would never be the same again. This moment, we all knew, was the end of something.

Behind me, Dad cleared his throat again.

As we drove away from our house for the last time, I twisted and looked out the back window of Orville's pickup at the small group of friends huddled in my front yard in the early morning sunlight. The three of them kept waving until we turned the corner, and then I twisted around on my seat and faced the direction we were going.

I sat up straight and watched my home town pass by outside the windows—Lawson Park, the school, the mall, the turn up Main Street and past the dark hobby shop with its big FOR LEASE sign, and then out past the fair grounds toward the highway. Dad drove slowly as we passed through town and none of us said anything. I knew we were all feeling the same way.

We pulled onto the highway, heading north, and the truck began to pick up speed. I felt my childhood slip behind me. I was heading on to a new stage of life—a new future—and I knew that God was going with me. He knows everything I ever need—even

before I do. I was His, and He'd never, ever forsake
me. I'd make new friends and settle into my new
school, and someday Cedarville would feel like home
to me.

　　But still, that sad lump lingered in my throat—
and I hoped that, miles behind us, huddled and shivering on my front lawn, the three best friends I would
ever have were still waving.

① iNVASiON from planet X
the misadventures of Willie Plummet

② submarine SaNDWiCHeD
the misadventures of Willie Plummet

③ ANYThiNG you can do I can do BeTTeR
Willie Plummet

④ ballistic BUGS
the misadventures of Willie Plummet

⑤ battle of the BANDS
Willie Plummet

⑥ Gold Flakes for Breakfast
the misadventures of Willie Plummet

⑦ TidaL Wave
Willie Plummet

⑧ Shooting sTARs
Willie Plummet

⑨ Hail to the CHUMP
the misadventures of Willie Plummet

⑩ The mONOpOly
the misadventures of Willie Plummet

⑪ Heads I wiN TaiLs you Lose
Willie Plummet

BUCHANAN & RANDALL

Look for all these **exciting WiLLiE PLuMMeT** *misadventures* at your local Christian **bookstore!**